PRAISE FOR THE

KINGSTON

— AND THE —

MAGICIAN'S LOST AND FOUND
DUOLOGY

★ "A fast-paced, magical read set in an accessible, vibrant world where Black magicians and a mainly Black cast take center stage."
—*Publishers Weekly*, starred review

"Intricately crafted twists at every turn keep the determined crew on their toes. The action is well paced, giving readers time to savor the myriad colorful characters who interact with the clue chasers . . . An enjoyable addition to most middle school mystery collections."
—*School Library Journal*

"Full of heart, magic, and mystery, this is the kind of book that makes you love books. Absolutely fantastic!"
—Sarah Beth Durst, award-winning author of *Catalyst*

"Readers who enjoyed *Kingston and the Magician's Lost and Found* will welcome this brisk sequel that maintains the engaging tone of the first series entry and entertainingly incorporates information about ancient Egyptian gods . . . An illuminating sequel."
—*Kirkus Reviews*

"Coded messages, characters who plainly know more than they're saying, doppelgangers, and secret schemes . . . all come together in a . . . breathlessly paced tale . . . Should leave readers even more delighted that the stage is set for sequels."
—*Booklist*

"Inventive, authentic, and razor-sharp, *Kingston and the Magician's Lost and Found* is at once an exhilarating fantasy and a moving tale of how far a father and son are willing to go for one another. Rucker Moses and Theo Gangi put aside familiar tropes to build something new, an underground New York City filled with magic and secrets, that challenges readers to solve its mysteries alongside its main character. As for Kingston, we've never seen anything like him—a young Black superhero determined to put the magic back in Brooklyn. He's sharp, feisty, funny, and always a step ahead. This is a special book, the kind that you fall in love with, because beneath the fun and twists, shining through is Kingston's big, bold heart." —Soman Chainani, *New York Times* bestselling author of The School for Good and Evil series

"[With] an engaging plot and history . . . this brisk first-person narrative will appeal especially to readers who like puzzles and illusions . . . A likable, otherworldly adventure with a bit of a mystery." —*Kirkus Reviews*

"The text is zippy and animated, reading more like a screenplay than a novel, and the secondary characters are splashy . . . Kingston is a carefully balanced mix of optimistic, jaded, and grief-stricken, moving through the world with more hope than the grown-ups who surround him." —*The Bulletin of the Center for Children's Books*

KINGSTON

AND THE

MAGICIAN'S LOST AND FOUND

KINGSTON

AND THE

MAGICIAN'S LOST AND FOUND

RUCKER MOSES
AND THEO GANGI

G. P. PUTNAM'S SONS

G. P. PUTNAM'S SONS

An imprint of Penguin Random House LLC, New York

First published in the United States of America by G. P. Putnam's Sons,
an imprint of Penguin Random House LLC, 2021
First paperback edition published 2022

Visit us online at penguinrandomhouse.com

THE LIBRARY OF CONGRESS HAS CATALOGED THE HARDCOVER EDITION AS FOLLOWS:
Names: Moses, Rucker, author. | Gangi, Theo, author. | Josselin, Sienne, illustrator.
Title: Kingston and the magician's lost and found / Rucker Moses and Theo Gangi;
map and interior illustrations by Sienne Josselin.
Description: New York: G. P. Putnam's Sons, [2020] | Summary: Returning to Brooklyn,
where his magician father disappeared years before, twelve-year-old Kingston learns
that magic is real and that if he enters the Realm, he might get his father back.
Identifiers: LCCN 2020027059 (print) | LCCN 2020027060 (ebook)
ISBN 9780525516866 (hardcover) | ISBN 9780525516873 (ebook)
Subjects: CYAC: Magic—Fiction. | Missing persons—Fiction. | Family life—Brooklyn
(New York, N.Y.)—Fiction. | Magicians—Fiction. | African Americans—Fiction.
Brooklyn—New York (State)—Brooklyn—Fiction. | Mystery and detective stories.
Classification: LCC PZ7.1.M67725 Kin 2020 (print) | LCC PZ7.1.M67725 (ebook)
DDC [Fic]—dc23
LC record available at https://lccn.loc.gov/2020027059
LC ebook record available at https://lccn.loc.gov/2020027060

Printed in the United States of America

ISBN 9780525516880

1 3 5 7 9 10 8 6 4 2

LSCH

Design by Suki Boynton • Text set in Warnock Pro

KINGSTON

AND THE

MAGICIAN'S LOST AND FOUND

MY FATHER WAS famous. He was the greatest magician in Echo City. And he made himself disappear.

Disappear. Like, here one second, gone the next.

Not *disappear* like he went out for milk and eggs and never came back, like the bullies at school used to say. He wasn't abducted by aliens or kidnapped by the mob. He doesn't have another family and he isn't dead.

He's alive. I know he is. No one else thinks so, but I know.

Ma says not to sit around waiting for him. That I'll just be disappointed. She's afraid I'll be like him, that I'll get lost in magic and she'll lose me like she lost him. I promise her I won't get lost. Sometimes she believes me.

Sometimes I mean it.

It's been four years, six months, and seven days since he's been gone. I was eight years old then. That's also four years and five months since we left Brooklyn, and today we're moving back to Pop's old home in Echo City, Brooklyn. Ma says the James Family Brownstone, aka 52 Ricks Street, will go back to the bank if we don't. She taught me a nasty-sounding word, *foreclosure*. It's like *closed* but times *four* and with a *ure* at the end in case you didn't know that the word meant business. Ma says it means banks take your house when you run out of money. So now she wants to open up a café, which is her lifelong dream.

But she's still nervous about moving. She doesn't say so, only I can tell by how she's driving. Inching along the hot summer streets and peeking at signs like a cat. Sighing at every red light. Squinting out the window at the street corners and row houses. She keeps tapping angry fingers at Google Maps on her phone screen. She thinks she knows Brooklyn, but it's been a while.

"I don't understand," she says, frustrated. "This thing has us jumping all over the streets."

Ma pulls the car over and flicks on the hazard lights of our rental SUV. She takes the phone off the dash mount, fingernails clicking on the screen as she stares with photon-beam focus. Mom believes in the power of apps and phone maps to get us places. The one thing she isn't doing is looking out the windows. But that's okay, I'm looking out for the both of us.

"How did our blue dot just land us in the middle of the Brooklyn Navy Yard?" she says. "Does it look like we're in the middle of the Navy Yard? Oh, wait now . . . now we're in the East River? We are literally in a body of water?"

I'm waiting for the car horns to start blaring at us, like they usually do when we stop and check directions, but there's no one around at all. It's like we found this one abandoned block in Brooklyn. I see a stop sign. There's a word scribbled underneath.

MAGIK

It makes me smile. Brooklyn and magic have always gone together for me. When we lived here with Dad, our lives were full of magic. Tricks, shows, and convos about the all-time great magicians filled our home back then. Before Dad disappeared and we left Brooklyn, and magic along with it. And Ma got so sick and tired of magic she didn't even want to hear about it anymore.

Then I realize the word *magik* is under the stop sign for a reason. It's a message.

STOP
MAGIK

"Well. Would you look at that," says Mom.

"Yeah. I know. 'Stop magik' sounds like good advice to you, right?"

Mom looks at me like she has no idea what I'm talking about.

"No—well, sure, I guess, but King, look—"

Before she can point her finger, I see it.

Looming right there above us like an elephant on the sidewalk.

The Mercury Theater.

We're quiet for a moment. I'm not sure how Mom will react.

I don't even know how I'm reacting, honestly.

Most times, when you visit a place you haven't seen in years, it seems small. Not the Mercury. And for sure I've grown a ton since I was here. But somehow the old theater is as huge as it ever was. It's like the dinosaur of buildings. Bigger than everything around it, and from another time.

Mom takes a deep breath and I hear her tremble on the exhale. My heartbeat is jacked up quick like I just hit the fast-forward button a couple times. I remember how sad she was, back when Pop never came home that first night. When she filled out the missing person report. How we held each other and cried.

I wonder if she's going to hit the gas and drive off, like she did the day we left Echo City. Like when she stashed all the pictures of Pops and his magic shows in a box down in the basement. I wonder if she's going to make a comment that cuts about magic and fools and leaving things in the past.

But she doesn't do any of that.

She opens her door and just stands there in the heat. Taking it in.

I hop out of the car and stand next to her. She doesn't look away from the theater, but her hand finds my shoulder.

There's a hole in the dome of the theater, with pigeons flying in and out. There are carvings of vines and grapes all up and down the columns and in patterns surrounding the windows, elaborate, with carved birds here and there fluttering at the stems. There are two gargoyles with mouths open and fangs tilted to the sky at the foot of the dome, like they're trying to shout to the world about the fire. Even now, all these years later, you can see the charred marks of that blaze.

To look at the marquee, you might think the theater was just down for a week between shows. Random letters are scattered around like they're waiting to be reassembled and make sense. But look at the glass front doors and those rusty chains, and you know that the shows, the crowds, the magic are all a distant memory. The ticket booth is boarded up with cheap plywood that couldn't even keep out the rain. The underside of the marquee is lined with busted-out light bulbs with shards like the stalactites of a cave.

Ma takes my hand. Crazy how many things she can say with a touch—things like, *I miss him, too*, *We're going to be okay*, and *I love you* and *You still better not be thinking about doing magic*.

But she doesn't say a word. And believe me, Ma can talk when she wants to.

We just stand there, holding hands, at the last place in this world anyone ever saw my father alive.

MOM GIVES MY hand one last squeeze and I understand it's time to get back in the car and move along.

Only I'm not ready. I'm *here*—Echo City, Brooklyn, the Mercury Theater—and I think of all the times I've fantasized about this place, all the late nights of imagining the theater in EC, BK, like it was some land of make-believe. In school I'd zone out and sketch that dome in the margin of my notebook without realizing. I'd remember the gargoyles in different poses and the vine carvings circling the windows like snakes.

I drift closer to the theater doors and I see my own reflection in the glass. Black eyes like little hovering planets.

Long cheeks and a double dimple like Pops. Hair tight at the sides, growing in free twists up top, several inches in the air like a volcano midblast. I've got a quiet face, I've been told. It stares back from the glass.

"King? King!"

Just a peek, I'm thinking.

Maybe there's a phantom crowd in there. Maybe the ghosts relive that night we lost him, over and over, like I do in my head. Maybe Pop left me some bread crumbs to follow. Maybe he left me a sign. Something to explain why he had to go.

"King!"

I use my hand like a visor and press the side of my palm against the glass and all the sun vanishes. I can just make out the inside.

Some corner of my mind thinks, *Maybe he's there.* Waiting, all these years. To reappear like this was all an elaborate trick, like, *ta-da.*

It's dark in there. Crazy dark. And behind all that dark there's . . . nothing. A whole lot of it.

"King! Get away from there, let's go!"

"It's fine, Ma!" I call back. "I'm coming!"

I linger there for a cool second that drags into a cool

five seconds and just as I'm ready, sorta, to pull myself away, I think I see something.

A dark figure in a Prince Albert coat.

I nearly leap out of my shoes.

It's just the outline of his shape in the reflection. It's a man. But he isn't in the theater. It's almost like he's trapped in the glass itself. I can't see his face in the dark. Just the coat, buttoned beneath the breast and cut off just before the knees, like something straight out of an old-school magic poster.

Is that him? In a throwback magician getup? Is it Pops?

"King? What is it? Will you get away from there?"

I glance at my mom. Then I press back against the glass, cupping my hands around my eyes to block out the sunlight.

Only, I don't see anything but the dark anymore. I stare as hard as I can at the nothing until Ma has her hand on my shoulder again, not quite so gentle this time. She spins me around to look at her.

"King, I said let's go. What are you doing?" Her eyes are wide with worry.

"Nothing, Ma. I just wanted to see."

"See what?"

See him.

"Nothing," I say.

"Please don't tell me I'm making a huge mistake bringing you back here," she says.

"No, Ma. It's good. I'm good. We good."

"Come on, King. Get in the car."

She looks at me with that side-eye and headshake like, *Look at this kid.*

Nuts like his father.

AS WE DRIVE away from the Mercury, I keep staring out
the back window. The theater doesn't appear abandoned
anymore—not exactly. Before, I thought the chains kept
the world *out*, but now I think they keep something *in*.
Something alive. As Mom takes a turn and the theater
passes out of sight, I think the chains expand for a second
like the ribs of a caged beast, breathing.

Now that we've found the Mercury, Mom knows
exactly how to get to our old brownstone. A few quick
turns and we pull up in front of the three-story town
house. I haven't seen this place since I was eight. It's not
how I remember it. Our stoop is overgrown with vines.
We used to decorate the windows of the storefront

"like a magician's Macy's," Pops would say. Now they're covered in old newspaper and the glass is cracked like spiderwebs. Tree roots carve up the sidewalk where my cousin Veronica used to school me at hopscotch.

The ground floor is a half-abandoned storefront. A rusty sign reads: SECOND SIGHT. A handwritten note is taped to a soiled window: *Possibly on Vacation*. There's a hodgepodge of locks on the door. Dead bolts, latches, chains, and a dozen or so knockers.

Mom sighs. "Well, we got three months to get this operation straight or the whole brownstone belongs to the Bank of Cities," she says.

"Sure, Ma, I know."

"And your uncles . . . ," she starts in. I've heard this one before.

"They're not really good at . . . *work*," we say at the same time.

"And 'Second Sight'?" Mom continues. "Is this a magic shop or are they selling eyeglasses here?"

"It's a reference," I say, and regret it right away.

"Do tell." Mom's eyes are wide.

I know I shouldn't explain. Mom gets tired of my magic history lessons. But I want to explain.

I close my eyes and speak extra fast. "Magician

Jean-Eugène Robert-Houdin's famous two-person mind-reading trick."

"Even a non-magic mom like me has heard of Houdini, you know."

"Not *Houdini*, it's Hou*din*," I correct her.

"So there's two *Houdies* now?" She chuckles.

"Houdini named himself after Houdin, that's all. He's only the father of modern magic."

"Why, thank you for the Kingsplanation." Her voice is dry.

"Yeah." I shrug. "I know stuff, is all."

"Yeah, you sure do. You even know a ton of stuff that *isn't* about magic. I'd love to hear about that stuff, too, sometime, how does that sound?"

"Sure, Ma." I do this sorta shrug-nod thing that Ma says looks like I got the hiccups.

"Welp, might as well try these knockers," she says, and taps one of the half dozen.

No answer.

I try my luck with a lion-faced knocker. The door rattles *rat-tat-tat*, with still no answer.

Ma spots a doorbell behind some overgrown ivy. But before her finger can find the button, the door swings open.

We're looking at the point of a sword blade.

Ma gasps.

A burnished-metal medieval helmet with grim eye slits glares from behind the curved blade.

"Aunt Nina?" a muffled voice echoes inside the helmet. "King?"

The warrior lowers the sword and raises the helmet visor.

It's my fourteen-year-old cousin, Veronica. Her soft brown eyes gaze at us. She pries the helmet from her head, which takes some effort, and shakes her hair out. Buzzed on one side and long the rest of the way around. Black with ash-blond streaks at the edges.

"I'm so sorry, I forgot you were coming today!"

"Veronica, if I may ask, you forgot we were coming, and you greeted us as if we were . . . *customers*?"

Veronica chuckles. "Oh. Those. Figured you were intruders. But customers—interesting. Suppose that's theoretically possible. Anyway, come in, come in! Experience the wonder," she says, oozing sarcasm.

My eyes adjust to the gloom as we enter a small room with red satin walls. It's all dusty. More like a museum than a shop. Masks and wands are set out on display. Shelves are lined with magic boxes, gag tricks, ornate coins, and top hats. I see a tuxedoed mannequin holding a fanned-out deck of cards. There's a set of fancy canes with brass handles in the shapes of different animal heads. Two taxidermy owls are mounted one on either side of a shelf: one perched, one in flight. There's photos of famous magicians on the walls. I recognize Dad's hero, Black Herman, as well as Jean-Eugène Robert-Houdin and the Martinka brothers, who opened the most famous magic shop in NYC. But this place is no Martinka & Company.

My Uncle Crooked Eye saunters into the room in an unbuttoned pink shirt with a greasy tank top underneath. His belly looks like it's made a nice home for pints of ice cream. He used to warm up the crowds for my pop with his Crooked Eye routine. He could move his wonky eyes in two different directions at the same time. He dubbed himself the "Ultimate Lookout."

I'm waiting for a trick to appear in his hand, or for his eyes to spaz out in whatever direction for a quick laugh. But he remains composed. "Nina! Darling, it's so good to see you."

"Heyward, it's good to see you, too," she says.

My uncle pauses. "Heyward," he repeats, like he's tasting the sound of it. "Well, I'll be, been years since anyone used my government name."

"Hi, Uncle Crooked Eye!" I announce.

His eyes roll around like a couple of cue balls until his pupils find me. Then they hit a split in opposite directions.

"Young King!"

He holds out a hand for me to slap and pulls me in for a hug. He crouches down and gives me a good once-over that lasts so long it's more of a twice-over.

"Well, well, looking more and more like him every day, Nephew," he says, almost to himself. Then he seems to remember that my mom is right there, and he buttons up like he didn't mean to mention Dad like that. "Except, you better looking, 'cause you look like your mama, too."

Mom chuckles at the lame attempt. "Smooth, Heyward."

She paces around the magic shop, eyeing the posters of old magic acts hung on the walls. There's an empty space between posters for Magician Mulholland and Okito the Great. Ma stops and stares.

"Now, I'm no detective," she says, "but how does dust settle on every inch of this place except for that perfectly rectangular bit on the wall right there?"

"Told you," says Veronica.

"That was Preston's poster, huh?" Ma asks Uncle Crooked.

I look to the empty spot on the wall and try to imagine my father's face there, drawn in full color like all those retro magic posters. I'm kind of disappointed that they took the poster down. I was looking forward to seeing King Preston the Great, at least in pictures, with that double-dimpled smile we share. Mom kept all our pics of Dad boxed up in the basement, where no one could see them. I wonder, *Doesn't anyone want to remember him?* Seems like even here in Brooklyn, in his old home in his hometown, folks want to pretend like he didn't exist.

Uncle Crooked tries to explain: "Well, Nina, thing is, we figured, you know, with you being away so long, that don't nobody want to be reminded of the past like that."

"It was discussed," says Veronica. "Whether to take it down or not. I thought you could handle it. I was overruled."

Ma smiles at Uncle Crooked. "Heyward, that's very considerate of you. But I'm okay. I can handle it. So can King. I mean, don't get me wrong, this place is heavy with the past. But we wouldn't have come back here if we weren't ready to face up to it," Mom continues. "My only question for you is—are you ready to let go?"

Uncle Crooked looks around the shop. He eyes every dusty trick, every old deck of cards with a look of love.

"Translation: he's not ready," says Veronica.

"How about you?" Mom asks her. "You up for helping turn this spot into the sweetest café in Echo City?"

"So ready, Auntie Nina. No offense, Uncle, but it's time to put this place to bed. Like, way past bedtime."

"Careful your father doesn't hear you talk like that," warns Uncle Crooked.

"Where is your brother? Is he around?" asks my mom, talking about my other uncle, Long Fingers, Veronica's father.

Veronica and Crooked Eye exchange a look.

"He's around," says Veronica.

"Let's just say he's attached to the . . . *magic* of this place," Crooked Eye explains carefully.

"Look, I get how much magic and this shop mean to you and your brother," says my mom. "But seriously, when was the last time you had a customer?"

"I can answer that for ya," Veronica says like she's about to enjoy this. She pulls a big dusty book from behind the counter and thumbs through the pages, half of them falling out of the binding. "Our last sale was March twentieth."

"Four months ago?" Mom asks.

"Actually . . . that was March twentieth of last year," Veronica says, looking more closely at the book.

Crooked Eye shrugs. "Was a good March."

"Heyward. It's time," says Ma.

Uncle Crooked sighs.

And I feel him. There's so much history in this store, these cards, books, and tricks. So many memories of Pop. Now Ma wants to clean him out of his old home. Like, I get that it's important to move on and all. But why does Mom have to be so good at it?

"Ma, can't we try and make the magic store work?" I ask. "I mean, maybe it needs a cleanup and to get some, you know, buzz or something?"

"Bees don't buzz that much," says Veronica.

"Thanks, Young King," Uncle Crooked says. "But your ma is right. In life, change is the one constant. Birth, death, life. Tide's in, tide's out. I appreciate what you're doing for us, Nina. I know you didn't have to come back here to save this place. But honestly, I can't imagine losing our home. On behalf of the James family, you have our thanks."

I touch the pocket watch that's hanging from my neck beneath my shirt.

It's a funny pocket watch that Pop left me. It's brass and old-fashioned and it goes all the way up to 13.

I touch it when I want to remember him.

Sometimes, I want to remember him most when I'm afraid he'll be forgotten forever.

MEET MY NEW room. Same as my old room.

I mean, literally the same room I grew up in.

Same mirror on the closet door as when I was eight.

There's something scary about mirrors. The way they make the world into more worlds.

My father disappeared into a mirror.

I know, that sounds weird. But it's true. I watched it happen and so did everyone else.

I knew in that moment that magic was real. Really real.

But then we moved out of Echo City and Mom started pretending that magic's not real. At school, they'd say that magic is not real. One time I got mad and told a teacher that I know magic is real, because my pop did magic and vanished through a mirror. Next thing I knew, Mom had to come meet the principal after school. I had to sit down with Gary, a counselor with curly hair and a beard, to "talk about my feelings." All we did was play chess, and I learned to pretend that Pops disappeared just like regular pops disappear.

Now that we're back in Brooklyn, I can stop pretending. I can be around my pop's folks, people like my uncles and V, who won't make me pretend and won't treat me like I'm crazy.

We're done moving in our boxes and stuff from the rental car, and Mom has lain down. I'm crazy restless and things are quiet—too quiet. I can almost hear the Mercury calling to me. I think about that figure in the Prince Albert coat in the dark, and I want to go back so bad it's like an ache in my neck. But there's no cool way to do it. No way to get out without Ma phoning missing persons for the second time in her life. No way to explore the city on my own.

So instead, I explore the house. Because if magic is hiding anywhere in this world, it's in a dusty old brownstone like this one, that's had a family of magicians living in it for decades.

In the kitchen, I find the wall where we used to mark how much I'd grown each year. I compare myself now to how short I was when I was eight. I've grown by about one full head—two if you count the twists in my hair. I was always on the tall side for my class, but not like Pop—he's the tallest of his brothers by far. When I first started growing out my twists, I liked how it made me taller, more like Pop.

The James Family Brownstone is basically how we left it. Most of the furniture is the same, but older. The one difference is that every spare space is stacked with books. Old books, new books, books with covers stripped off, books with crumbling bindings, or with titles so faded you can barely read them. Stacks and stacks of them load the hallways, windowsills, and half the upstairs bathtub. I'm searching the house looking for magic, and instead my neck hurts from holding my head sideways trying to read all the titles of these books on and about magic, like *Black Herman's Secrets of Magic, Mystery and Legerdemain*, and *The Fourth Book of Occult Philosophy*. The bookcase in the living room is also loaded with books, but here they're all ordered neatly, covering the entire back wall, floor to ceiling, with a rolling ladder like in a legit library. I scan the bindings—*Picatrix, Testament of Solomon*—and recognize one title in particular, *The Four Elements of Magic*, by Anonymous.

I remember Pops used to read that book so much, Mom would make comments like, "*The Four Elements of Magic*? Much as you read that book, more like *The Fourth Member of Our Family*." I wish I had asked Pops about the elements. Maybe I was just too young, or before he disappeared I wasn't as curious about magic.

Cracks run down the faded leather spine like the lines on my palm. I try to pull the book from the shelf but feel this strange tension, like a pair of fingers is holding the book from the other side. I pull against the resistance, and the book slides halfway off the shelf as a hinge somewhere inside the wall seems to move. I hear a crank and grinding of gears and at first I think I've broken something.

Then the entire bookcase rattles in its grooves and slowly turns inward, revealing an opening.

Wow, I think, and I wonder, *Was this always here?*

Did Pops use this passage, and I never knew?

I step into a small foyer that's the shape of a hexagon. There's the entrance to my back, the other side of the bookcase that closes behind me. There's a hallway in front of me. And on the four walls to my right and my left, there's nothing but pictures and clippings of Pop.

It's like a shrine. Three of the walls are dedicated to

his best tricks. There's Hooker's Vanishing Deck on one wall, the trick where he could make cards disappear and reappear, and that no one could ever figure out. There's the Skull of Balsamo—that creepy, hovering human skull with a brass jaw that could see into the past and speak to the dead. Then there's William Tell's Pistol, the act with the old-style handgun that shot a bullet Pop could catch like a fastball. The fourth wall is all clippings about his strange disappearance, and photos of the Mirror.

Looking at these walls, I realize how much Pop is missed. He's not just missed by that old, forgotten magic store out front—he's like the glue that held this place together. And I finally get to look at pictures of him. I scan every feature in every frame, looking for faces that I make and poses that I hit, too.

The doorway that leads to the hallway has an inscription hung over top:

THE FOUR ELEMENTS OPEN THE WAY.

I shrug. Guess I figured out that one on my own.

I walk through and there's some lived-in rooms. There's a sofa with a kitchen at the back.

Through another doorway, I find the jackpot.

Well, not *the* jackpot. But *a* jackpot. Not real magic exactly, but a real magician's workshop.

The walls are lined with shelves overflowing with screws, light bulbs, springs, bolts, crystals, bones, cigar boxes, magician's wax, bent cards, and old newspapers. Projects are everywhere. Half-finished or half-abandoned, depending on your point of view. Half-completed sketches. Over a half dozen moldy coffee cups. Neon lights in odd shapes cast a strange color across the room.

And my Uncle Long Fingers sits right in the center of it all, working on something that's covered beneath a giant tarp.

I stay quiet and watch him work, though I can't make out what's under there. Uncle Long still hasn't noticed me, he's so into his project, fingers bent around a screwdriver like spider legs. The focus he pours into the end of his working fingertips is a physical force. Probably has its own gravitational field.

Uncle Long Fingers has let himself go. He sports a matted 'fro like a shrub that needs a gardener. His bushy salt-and-pepper beard is speckled with crumbs. His body is soft and sunken as a beanbag chair. But his mind—you can see the intelligence, wild in his eyes like an electric storm.

I inch closer, trying to get a look at what he's working

with, what he's screwing or unscrewing or fixing or taking apart.

Something familiar catches my eye. A pocket watch dangles from a hook that's attached to a plaque. I look closer and realize it's just like the watch my dad left me—it goes all the way up to 13. There's a bunch of random letters scrawled on the wall above the plaque:

Ybbx Sbejneq naq Onpxjneq, Vg'f Nyy gur Fnzr

"What's up, Nephew?" His gruff voice startles me nearly out of my skin.

"H—hi, Uncle," I say, and wave a hand.

But waving at him is pointless. He still hasn't looked up at me.

"You lost?" he asks.

"No," I say firmly. My eyes fall back to the scrawl of letters that looks like total gibberish—or, I should say, the code. *"Look Forward and Backward, It's All the Same,"* I recite.

He strokes the crumbs from his beard and runs his fingers over the hodgepodge of letters like he's impressed. "You can decode those letters that fast?" he asks.

I reach for the chain around my neck and show him the watch.

"My dad taught it to me. He left me one just like the one you got here."

Long Fingers takes both watches in his hands and examines them together. "Well, I'll be. That's Preston's old watch, all right," he says with a whisper. Then he glances at me and recovers his gruff expression. "Never knew he gave this to you."

"He used to write me notes in that code to see how long it would take me to figure it out. He told me how time is just a construct of the mind. The ability to slow down and speed up time is the magician's greatest asset. A trained magician can see the smallest blink of an eye. The key is thirteen," I say, and point to the number 13 on the watch.

"Oh yeah?" He smirks. "So you got it all figured it out?"

"It's a simple code. You take a letter, and substitute it with another letter that's thirteen letters forward or thirteen letters back. You get the same letter whether you go forward or backward."

I grab a piece of paper and a pencil from his messy desk and write it out.

"So take the letter *A*, right? In the code, the letter *A*

is repped by the letter N, because an N is thirteen ahead of A," I say, scribbling down letters and numbers. "Or you can count thirteen back and start with Z. It's all the same. A is always N. It doesn't matter, because, *Look forward and backward . . ."*

"It's all the same." Long Fingers finishes the phrase. "Not bad, kid. Time is the key. Look forward and backward *in time."*

He reaches to the plaque and removes a wood-grain slat, revealing two circular sets of letters surrounding the clockface. Clearly, he made this plaque just to mount his or my dad's Watch of 13. The alphabet runs in two concentric circles around the numbers on the clockface, showing how the code works. The first set starts with an *A* over the 1 on the clock, the second set starts with an *N* over the 1.

"Wow, this thing has been around my neck for four years and I never knew that trick. My dad always made me do the math."

"I suspect that was part of your daddy's point. We came up with that little code back in the day, passing notes to each other. But you knew that phrase already. You didn't decode it that fast, did you?" he asks, genuinely curious.

I shrug with a wink. "Magician's secret."

But of course he's right.

"Okay, Nephew, color me impressed. You know the code, you figured out the bookcase and made it to my little lab here. So what brings you snooping around this old house?"

"Magic."

"Magic? Haven't you heard? We gettin' rid of that stuff so we can serve coffee and biscuits," he says with a bitter growl.

"I don't mean that magic. Not those tricks out there. Anyone with a few bucks can buy those. I mean real magic."

"What makes you think there's any such thing as real magic?"

"'Cause I seen it," I say. I give him a cold look so he knows what I mean.

"Ah. Yeah, well, I think you seen enough of that stuff to last a lifetime."

"No. I want to see more."

"Maybe you don't know what it is you want."

"Of course I don't know. How could I know? My ma doesn't want me talking or thinking about magic. She just wants me to be a normal boy. But I don't think there's any such thing as that, and if there was, normal boys don't see their fathers vanish into mirrors."

He shrugs. "Maybe not."

"I have questions, Uncle."

"Well, you can ask them, but just so we clear, that don't mean I got to answer them."

"Fine."

I want to ask about the Mercury and the figure in the Prince Albert coat—but I've made lists of questions, all for a moment like this, and a random one awkwardly jumps out at me. "If magic is real, why don't we magic the dishes clean every night?"

He laughs. "That's the best you got?"

"How come we don't magic the house out of fore-closure?"

He pauses and gives me a serious look. "Clearly, it doesn't work like that, 'cause you here with your mama, isn't that right, Nephew?"

"How come we don't magic Pop back?"

Uncle Long shakes his head and goes back to his work. "Go find your mama before I tell her you back here shoving wet fingers in electrical sockets."

"You can't say? Or you don't know?"

"I said *get*," he growls.

"Does that mean we can't do it? Or we can, but you don't want to?"

"Get!" he barks like an old dog about to bite.

I take a couple last looks at his workshop on my way out.

But nothing's floating, glowing, burning, shattering, reassembling, vanishing, or reappearing.

Just a bunch of broken-down parts and half-baked tricks.

No magic.

At least none that I can see.

THE NEXT DAY, Saturday, from the crack of dawn, Ma has her trusty vacuum cleaner humming. I call the machine Ole Betsy. Sounds like she's gargling lug nuts in a cast-iron throat, as usual.

I open my bedroom door to find Ma running Ole Betsy on the hallway carpet.

"Oh, King, good, you're up," she says.

"Huh?" I cup my hand to my ear.

Ma gets the idea and shuts off Betsy. "How'd you sleep?" she asks.

"Okay, I guess."

I see over her shoulder into her room. Her bed is

already made up all perfect, corners tucked crazy tight like they do in hotels.

"How about you?"

When Ma is worried about stuff, she likes to keep busy and work. That's how I know she must be worried. About the café or just being here with all these memories, I can't say.

"Wanna help make breakfast?" she asks.

We go from making breakfast with Uncle Crooked to cleaning the kitchen with V and waiting for Long Fingers to come down and eat (he never does) to clearing the table to unpacking all our moving boxes and right into boxing up the magic shop in those same boxes. It's tough for Uncle Crooked Eye, but Mom tries to be as gentle as she can. Uncle Crooked is at one point standing in the corner, arms full of tricks he can't possibly part with, like a kid clutching his favorite stuffed animals. Veronica gets him to demonstrate this trick where he blindfolds himself, and Ma and I are able to work.

By 3:00 p.m. it's scorching hot both inside and out. The AC unit chugs in the corner but isn't much help. We all retreat to the kitchen and break for a snack. But I'm still starving. Around 4:30 p.m., the air conditioner goes out. V and I make such a fuss about the heat that Ma lets me go out for some pizza. Veronica doesn't need to beg or even ask permission, but for some reason she does anyway, almost like she wants to. Ma makes a crack about how us "young ones can't take the heat" and gives me a couple bucks for a slice.

———⟶———

AT 5:00 P.M., when we get outside, the sun is still intense. Sunset is a long ways off on our block.

Looking around Ricks Street, I remember Pop all over this place. On our stoop with his collar open, in linen pants and a porkpie hat. Ma always called him "timeless." He didn't dress like anyone else on the block. He also didn't let me waste the day away on an iPad. Sundays were for learning magic. Coins, cards, watches, we'd sit outside and do it all. Pops knew everyone. I remember him by the gate asking the neighbors about their older folks (Mom would ask about the babies). I see the NO PARKING sign where my bike was stolen one time, and Pop just had to say a couple words to a couple people and, by the morning, the bike reappeared chained to that same post. I see the bodega where they'd save newspapers or flyers with Dad's shows.

The sidewalk is a patchwork of odd rectangles, from spackled gray to black tar to blond concrete, with sprouts of yellow grass in the cracks between. The gaps get even bigger by the trees, where the roots beneath crack the concrete and stone. I remember Pop would put a hand over those special stones, rising from the earth like the undead, and say, "There's more life under there. There's magic under there," with that wink like maybe he was joking.

I notice some words written in pink and yellow chalk on the concrete. They read:

Are you hurting?

Are you helping?

Am I hurting? Am I helping? The questions worm into my mind.

Then I realize I'm not exactly sure what the questions mean.

"Hey, V," I say, and point to the sidewalk. "You think that means *Are you hurting?* like, are you sort of hurting others, like other people? Or you think it means *Are you hurting?* like, are you in pain?"

She looks, reads, and smiles. "Maybe it's however you take it to mean. Like, it depends on the person."

We walk some more in silence and pass more faded chalk letters on the sidewalk, too faded to read. Veronica has a hand on her sore hip from all that work at the house. She was always older and bigger than me, but now she's a teenager and has, like, teenage muscles and this walk that makes me think she could beat me up if she wanted. I realize how little I know about her these days. If she was hurting about something, other than her hip, I'd have no idea what it was.

"Well, what does it mean for you?" I ask.

"It means both, I guess. If you're in pain, you're probably hurting someone else. And if you're helping yourself, you're probably helping others. But it's interesting, how everyone takes it different. How'd you take it?" she asks. "Like, what's the first thing you thought when you first read the questions?"

"Oh, I don't really remember."

"You don't remember? It was seven seconds ago. What was your first thought?" she asks.

"Um . . ."

"Your very first thought," she says rapid-fire, "right away—go!"

"Okay, well, honestly, my first thought, my very first thought, before I thought about what the words really mean, was, like, it's great being back here, but I miss Pop. And it hurts."

"Oh," she says. "Sorry."

"Yeah. It's okay. You asked."

"Lots of reminders of him?"

"Yup. Everywhere I look," I admit. "It's thick with him around here."

"Okay, well, let me ask you this. Are you helping?"

"Well, sure, I helped unpack and organize and—"

"No, I mean, are you helping yourself feel better about missing your pop?" she asks.

I open my mouth to answer before I realize I have no idea what to say. I want to say, *Why, yes, I'm helping in all of these helpful ways,* but I got nothing.

I say, "To be honest, I don't even know what helping would look like. Unless I went back in time and stopped him before he went through the Mirror at the Mercury."

"What?" she says, her eyebrows bent like crowbars. "No, I mean, helping yourself, like, to not miss him so much."

"How is that even possible? Like, I miss him. That's how I feel."

"Right, but we can help ourselves still, right? Sorta help ourselves not feel so bad about things we can't change."

"Only thing that would make me feel better is if he were here," I say.

Veronica wants to say something else, probably about accepting things the way they are, but I think my tone tells her not to bother.

"So what," she says, "you expect him to just appear out of thin air?"

I shrug. "He disappeared into thin air. Why not? I mean, V—you ever go by that old theater?"

"Why would I go over there?"

"I don't know. Is it really abandoned?" I ask.

"Well, I think there's some pigeons squatting in the hole in the roof. Does that count?"

"I mean . . . I don't know. It's stupid. Forget I said anything."

"Done. 'Cause you didn't say anything," she says, and looks at me like I've got five heads.

"What I mean to say is, does any magic stuff sorta happen over there? Or anywhere, in general, I guess."

Veronica laughs. "'Does any magic stuff sorta happen?'" She imitates me, but I know my voice doesn't sound that squeaky. "King, cuzzo, what sorta magic stuff are you imagining?" Now she's really cheesing.

I realize how close that smile is to mine, and Pop's.

"Why are you acting like this is some crazy question? Like, we know my pops vanished in a mirror. That's what

I'm imagining, V. Magic stuff like what we all saw with our own eyes."

Her smirk softens and her smile is genuine. "Listen, I feel for you, I really do. I mean, I was raised without my mom, and that's really hard sometimes. And my dad won't tell me anything about her, just that she didn't care enough to raise me."

"Ouch. That's what he says?"

"That's exactly how he says it, too." Veronica bites her lower lip and it disappears beneath her teeth. I remember how she used to make that worried face a lot when she was much younger. "But *her*—I miss her sometimes, is that weird? Like, how can you miss someone you can't even remember? But I do."

We walk in silence for a while, missing our missing parents.

But I'm also thinking about how she didn't answer my question.

I REMEMBER WALKING up and down Thurston Avenue with Dad. We had a routine. First the French Drop—a coffee shop with all these strange taxidermied animals mounted to the walls. It's another bodega now. Then we'd hit Harry's Handcuffs Hardware and buy what most people considered junk. Pops said it was a gold mine. He usually had a list from Long Fingers, always the weirdest stuff: doorknobs, mannequins, springs, fabric, circuit boards, old gutted TVs, car parts, even pigeons. The last stop was Not Not Ray's Pizza, best (and only) slice in Echo City.

Pop would explain how there's like one thousand Ray's Pizza places all around NYC. Famous Ray's, Original Ray's, Famous Original Ray's Pizza. So somebody opened a spot in Brooklyn called Not Ray's Pizza. So when Matteo Spinelli opened his spot in Echo City, he called it Not Not Ray's Pizza. To avoid confusion.

As we stroll the block, I see that Not Not Ray's has stood the test of time.

This place. I remember the heat-crust-and-cheese smell of the oven wafting outside. Smells so good it hits your toes. We enter and in the back there's dough being tossed in the air like flying saucers. But I can barely see Matteo Spinelli because there's this really tall kid there standing in the way. He's all rods and elbows, like scaffolding.

"Come on, Matty-o, just a couple of those pepperonis. I got you for them tomorrow."

The kid's voice sounds strangely familiar . . .

"First of all, my ginormous friend, it's pronounced *Matteo*," he says in a strong Brooklyn-Italian accent, "and you still owe me for the extra sausage from last week."

"Come on, Matty—*Matteo*—I'm a growing boy, my body needs those toppings."

"And my cash register needs that dollar fifty. Look at you, you've had enough toppings, you bang yer head in my doorway every other day."

"Yes, and that reminds me that you, sir, will be hearing from my personal injurious lawyer. Or I can accept a settlement of six to seven pepperonis on this slice right here."

"Next?" Matteo says to us. "Hi, Veronica. Can I help you?"

The tall kid turns around and I recognize his face. He lights up with a one-thousand-gigawatt smile.

"King! The King is back!" he shouts.

He holds out an open hand, fingers long as ski poles.

"Eddie?" I say.

"They call me Too Tall nowdays," he says.

I get a pain in my neck looking up at him.

"Oh yeah?" I say, blocking the light fixture from my eyes. "What they call you that for?"

"Um . . . ," he says, and taps a finger to his lips.

Then he sees my expression and busts out laughing.

"My man, Young King!" he says, and slaps my palm and pats my back. He holds my hand and looks at me like he's seeing a ghost.

My hand disappears inside his massive one like a coin trick.

Coin trick . . . Makes me think of something.

"Kingston?" asks Matteo Spinelli.

Matteo Spinelli is just as I remember him. The only

thing he liked better than pizza was a good magic trick. Show him one he hadn't seen, and you could snag a free slice.

"Matteo, you remember my cousin?" asks Veronica.

"Of course I do, Preston's kid. Welcome back!"

"Matteo, you still giving out slices for a good magic trick?" I ask him.

"I don't know, my friend. I haven't seen a trick in four years."

I have these trick white magician's gloves that Uncle Crooked Eye let me hold, since they fit me so well. I slide them out of my back pocket and pull them on. Too Tall Eddie's coins sit on the counter. I scoop them up in these white gloves and cup my hands over them and start shaking them like maracas.

"Eddie—"

"Too Tall," he corrects me.

"Too Tall, how much money was here before?"

"Two dollars, twenty-five cents," he says.

"Matteo, is that right?" I ask, still shaking the coins in my gloved hands.

"Yup. A dollar fifty short for a pepperoni slice."

Too Tall rolls his eyes.

Veronica, onto what I'm up to, winks at Matteo.

"Okay. Matteo, hold out your hands, please?"

I dump the coins into Matteo's palms.

The pizza shop owner counts the coins twice, three times, and nods, impressed, as he slides them into his register. "One pepperoni, coming right up, and a free slice for the young magician!"

Too Tall's eyes *wow* in amazement. He points a finger at my chest as a smile expands across his face. "You, my man, you are magic. You are a magical little individual."

"So, Too Tall—"

"King, you can call me Tall, for short," he says with a warm, pepperoni-filled grin. Too Tall, Veronica, and I are all sitting in a booth with our slices.

"I ain't calling you nothin' for *short*," I say with a snort.

"Good one!" he says.

Veronica shakes her head. "How did you two dorks survive without each other all these years?"

"That's a good question," Tall says, taking her words at face value. "I played a lot of basketball. Got going on my sneaker collection, and when I couldn't afford a slice at Not Not Ray's, I ate a lot of peanut-butter-and-honey sandwiches."

"Really?" I say. "Interesting. Honey, you say?"

"Honey." He nods. "Jelly is not a necessary condiment. The important thing is the sweet, mixed with the nut butter." He chef-kisses his fingertips.

"Well, how does this sound?" I suggest. "Jelly-with-cream-cheese sandwiches."

Too Tall's eyes go wide.

"On cinnamon-raisin bread," I add.

"Mind. Blown."

Veronica hits an eye roll strong enough to flip th checkered pizza table. "Okay, you two are the worst. thought boy talk would be more interesting than this."

"Thought wrong, cuzzo," I say with a satisfying bi Not Not Ray's finest.

"So what you been up to all these years?" asks T;

"Just, you know, going to school, and working magic."

"Working on your magic? Like, how you w jump shot?"

"Sorta like that, I guess."

"Like—magic *tricks*?" Tall asks.

"No, not stupid magic *tricks*." Veronica j eyes of mischief. "Real magic. Right, King?"

"What? No, Tall was right, magic trick

Veronica goes on: "So what were you asking me about just now? About the Mercury and magic 'stuff'?"

"Well, yeah, that's different—"

"*Real magic*, right, King? That's what you were wondering about?"

I set my slice down on the wax paper and wipe the grease from the corners of my mouth. Too Tall's and Veronica's eyes are on me. I remember their faces from years before, how they used to look. Veronica's eyes were wider then, her cheeks chubbier, her smile was full of teeth too big for her mouth. Too Tall—we used to call him "Skinny Eddie"—and, well, there's about twice as much of him now. That was also a different me then, and I start thinking about time, and how different I was four years ago before the fire at the Mercury. Before Dad vanished. Before I knew for certain that magic was really real.

"I was asking Veronica about the Mercury Theater. Where they had the fire. Where my dad disappeared. I mean, you been around Echo City all this time. You ever seen anything go down over there?"

"Any *magic* stuff?" Veronica chimes in with that sarcastic grin.

Too Tall thinks this over. "You mean that old building with the big dome and those gargoyles?"

"That's the one."

"Well . . . this is going to sound weird, but . . ." Tall hesitates.

"Tall, my father disappeared through a mirror four years ago and never came back. You're not going to out-weird me."

Too Tall is startled to hear this. "What? What do you mean, *through a mirror*?"

This leaves me speechless.

I always figured that everyone knew that Dad was gone, but it never occurred to me that everyone might not know *how* Dad had gone.

Maybe the real story went around—but who would believe that?

"He's not lying," says Veronica, sincere for once. "I was there. Everyone saw it, right there onstage. Kingston's dad jumped in that creepy Mirror and was just *gone*. There was a big crash, and then that fire everywhere. Last time anybody saw him."

"Whoa," says Too Tall. "So when you left? Okay . . . Wow."

The expression on his face seems to work out a whole lot of missing information about a whole lot of missing years.

"So what were you going to say?" I ask. "About the Mercury?"

"Oh, the theater? Nothing. Just I heard, my one cousin told my other cousin and he told—"

"Told you?" asks V.

"No, he told this kid I ball with on the playground, and he told my closest cousin, who told me that one of those gargoyles ate a pigeon one time. But you were right. Your story, that's way weirder."

"A gargoyle ate a pigeon?" I ask.

"Well, either that or the pigeon just flew away. The details get lost in translation. But go back to the part about your pops and the Mirror. I'd heard that he got a show in Vegas and you guys all left, after the fire."

"Who told you that?" asks Veronica.

"One of my cousins. I can't remember which one." Tall shakes his head. "*Man*, I'm sorry to hear you had to go through that. You ever think he might come back? I mean, if he could disappear, why not reappear, you know?"

Veronica nods. "I think that's why he was asking about the Mercury. Is that right, King?"

"Yeah," I admit. "I mean, he's a magician, right? And all magicians' great tricks have a finale. It's called the Prestige, where they show the audience the card they pulled, or—"

"Or the rabbit they pulled out of the hat?" Tall chimes in helpfully.

"Sure. There's that moment when the audience is wowed and the magician—he stands there and takes a bow. And there was this old magician named Black Herman. He did this trick where he'd bury himself alive and then, three weeks later, folks would buy tickets to watch him dig himself out, then follow him to the stage for a show. And he was one of my pop's heroes. I just can't help but think maybe . . ." I let my words trail off. For some reason I can't bring myself to say the rest out loud.

Veronica steps in. "Maybe this is a disappear-reappear trick, with a four-year delay on the Prestige?"

Hearing her say the words makes me wince. I look at Too Tall, though, and he doesn't think it sounds so strange.

"Maybe your father's doing the Black Herman move?" he suggests.

"Maybe?" I say.

"Well, there's one way to find out, li'l King. Now, I'm as creeped out by burnt-up old-timey theaters with daddy-stealing mirrors as anyone, but let's go check this place out, and see if there isn't a magic Pops waiting to appear onstage."

"For real?" I say.

"For reals. Tired of running these fools in pickup games at the playground all day anyway. Plus, it's too hot for that mess. Let's go check out this theater."

I'm looking at Veronica. I expect her to shoot down our stupid idea and send us back to Ma.

But instead she says, "Hey, tall guy, let me ask you something. Are you hurting, or are you helping?"

Too Tall is confused by her question. "I have hurt exactly no one. Why? What have you heard?"

Veronica shrugs and says to me, "I don't know, King. He sounds guilty about something."

Too Tall looks bewildered. He turns and says to me, "King, what is she talking about?"

"Somebody wrote *Are you hurting? Are you helping?* on the sidewalk by our house," I say. "And now she's asking people, I guess?"

"You were the one obsessed with it," V grumbles.

"I'm helping!" Tall insists.

"I believe you," I say to Tall.

"Good. You should," he says.

"How about you, V?" I ask. "You helping, or hurting? Are you coming, or staying?"

She holds up her hands in surrender. "You gonna finish that crust before we go or nah?"

WE'RE UNDER THE marquee in front of the once-
majestic entrance of the Mercury Theater. The chains
roped around the doors seem to grind and tighten. The
shade beneath the sign feels like the sort of gloom where
ghosts gather. The shattered glass bulbs hang above us
like they could drop at any moment. I step up to the glass
and peer through. I'm looking for that figure in the Prince
Albert coat. All I see is darkness.

"One thing I never understand is creepy gargoyles,"
says Too Tall. "Like, why would anyone put those
crazy-lookin' demon-monsters up there in the first
place?"

I look up to the stone-carved creatures. Their eyes

are round and bulging above snarling fangs and forked tongues, long like frozen snakes. "I don't know," I say.

"I like them," says Veronica.

"You do?" asks Tall.

"Yeah. They look like they dine on human hearts or something," she says like that's a good thing.

"Just what I was thinking," Too Tall mumbles.

I'm waiting for one to spring to life. "Maybe they're supposed to be, like, guarding something."

My eyes then drift to the random letters left splashed on the marquee. Something feels off about them.

"Why do you suppose those letters are like that?" I ask.

Veronica squints up. She reads, "*O-E-V-P-X* . . . *J-N-Y-Y* . . . Seems pretty good and nonsensical to me."

"Yeah. I mean, isn't that weird?" I say. "Shouldn't it say something like 'Magic Show,' but with letters missing?"

"Like, 'Mgi how'?" says Tall.

"Yeah. Or something. I mean, why those letters?"

Veronica stares at the sign. "Like, I can't tell what the sign ever said. Strange, since the theater hasn't been touched since the fire."

"Exactly," I say. "It's almost like somebody got up there and put those letters—specifically those letters—like that. I wonder? Nah, it's too crazy."

"You wonder what, King?" says Veronica.

"Look forward and backward, it's all the same," I say, almost to myself.

"Um, you want to try making some sense to us here on the planet Earth?" says V.

"There's this code my dad taught me. In fact, your dad told me they came up with it together."

"You talked to my dad?" Veronica asks, astonished.

"Well, yeah. I found his workshop, you know? And he had this watch there." I take out the pocket watch from around my neck. "It goes up to the number thirteen, just like mine."

Tall and Veronica check out the numbers going all the way around.

"It's kind of cool, how it looks like a normal watch face, then it's like, no, the numbers go to thirteen, not twelve, and that knocks the three, six, and nine off-center," says Too Tall.

"See, thirteen—it's like half of twenty-six, the number of letters in the alphabet. So to crack the code, you take the numeric value of each letter, and either add or subtract by thirteen. Then that's the decoded letter. Make sense?"

"Not really," says Tall.

"And your father taught you this?" asks Veronica.

"Well, yeah. You ever see that watch to thirteen your dad has in his workshop?"

"Honestly, I never go in there. Like, never."

"My pops used to write me notes in the code," I say, and I take in the random letters on the marquee once more. "Anybody have a pen and paper?" I ask.

"We're in the middle of the street, dude, not class," says Too Tall. "I got a phone, that help?"

"I don't think so. Think I need to draw on something."

"How about this?" Veronica digs in her pocket and comes up with two ground-down sticks of chalk, one pink, one yellow.

"Okay, wait a minute . . . ," I say. "*You* write that stuff on the sidewalk?"

She shrugs. "Keeps people honest."

"Okay, wow. Well, why didn't you say anything?"

"It was fun watching you think it through when you thought it was a message from beyond. Now come on, cuz, show me this code."

I take the chalk and draw a circle on the sidewalk. I don't think anyone will mind. Then I imagine the circle like my watch and put the number 13 at the top, and draw each number counting all the way around. "Okay, so here's the Watch of 13. With me so far?"

"Right there with you," says Tall.

"Then you go around with the alphabet," I continue, and I write an *A* beside the 1, a *B* beside the 2, and all the way to the *M* beside the 13.

"Okay," says Tall, "looks like you ran out of numbers for letters."

Veronica smirks like she's getting it.

"Right, then you finish the alphabet around the circle like this," I say, and keep writing another row of letters around the last row. So now the *A* has an *N* beside it, the *B* has an *O* beside it, all the way to the *M* that has a *Z* beside it, above the number 13. "The code works where you just sub one letter for the one beside it. So the first letter on the marquee is *O*, so sub that with a—"

"*B!*" Tall says, looking

at the sidewalk drawing, and he shoots a fist up like he hit a buzzer beater.

"Not bad, cuzzo," says Veronica. *"Look forward and backward."* She repeats the phrase I mentioned earlier.

"It's all the same," I say. "Right. If you go clockwise or counterclockwise, the code letter is thirteen letters away, forward or backward. It's all the same."

"Okay, okay, I like this now," says Tall. "Next?"

We decode the rest of the letters, and Too Tall types them up on his cell phone as we go.

O = B
E = R
V = I
P = C
X = K

As the first word begins to form, my fingers tremble with adrenaline.

O-E-V-P-X from the marquee becomes *B-R-I-C-K*.

"Brick," says Veronica.

"Brick?" says Tall.

"Brick," I repeat. "Well, it makes more sense than *oevpx*, anyway. Let's keep going."

The last four letters:

J = W
N = A
Y = L
Y = L

W-A-L-L.
"Looks like we've hit a brick wall," Too Tall cracks.
"Ba-dum-bum," says Veronica.
I stare at the words Too Tall has typed up on his screen.
"This is crazy," says Veronica. "I mean, you realize what this means?"
"That someone who knows the code put those letters up there like that? Yeah, V. That's, like, all I can think of. I mean, the only people who know that code are my father and yours. And Crooked Eye, I suppose."
"That we know of . . . ," says V.
"True . . . But then, what's this message mean?"
"Has to mean something," says Veronica.
I pace and tap a finger to my skull.
"Does putting your finger on your head really help you think or nah?" asks Veronica.
But I ignore her.

Brick wall . . . Brick wall . . . must be a reference . . .

"Got it!" I shout. "It's a trick!"

"What's a trick? It's not really a brick wall?" says Too Tall.

"Sorta. It's a classic Houdini trick. Houdini's Brick Wall. He'd fool the audience into thinking he'd walked through a solid brick wall by escaping through a trapdoor covered by a carpet in front."

And there I see it—a little ways down from the chained-up doors, there's a moldy old rug lying by the exterior wall.

I rush to it and throw it back.

There's a small chute tunneling under the theater.

"Pop," I whisper.

"You're not for real going down in there, right, King?" Too Tall asks in a shaky voice.

By the time he finishes his question, he's got his answer.

I slide in, feetfirst.

The light from the summer city day vanishes as I plunge down the throat of the chute.

THE CHUTE TAKES me down a ways, then switches directions, like gears somewhere have moved the chamber around. There's a sudden drop directly down, and I finally land in absolute darkness.

I call out to Veronica and Too Tall.

I hear bodies sliding down the chute above me, and muffled yells. Gears move again from the upper levels. I step out of the way, hoping they'll come after me, but they never show.

Then it's quiet again.

I wonder if the chute took them somewhere different.

Wish I had Tall's phone.

Wish Ma had let me have a phone already.

Wish I had light, I mean any sort of light.

And eventually, I think, *What am I even doing here?*

I shout some more for Tall and Veronica, but my words seem to bounce right back, like wherever I am, there's layers of hard, old metalwork that likes sound about as much as it likes light.

I turn and try to climb back up the chute, but the opening is closed now. I press my fingers against the grime of metal and there's no give.

It seems there's only one way to go, and that's forward.

Once, I would have been so psyched to be in the bowels of the Mercury Theater, free to explore. But this dark is so dark it's *weird.* I hold my hand out in front of my face, waiting for my eyes to adjust and hoping to make out the shape of my fingers—the fingers I know are right there . . .

But nothing. I can't even see my own hand.

So I walk, and trust—no, hope—that my outstretched hand will stop anything from hitting my face before my face hits it.

The floor feels uneven beneath my feet, gravelly and dusty. I kick something squishy and hope it doesn't have fur, a tail, and a heartbeat. I blink and blink and begin to see things. Or think I see things.

My hand hits something. An old metal rod, by the feel of it—rusty, but sturdy, like a fire escape. It's hovering at about eye level. I give the rod a good shake, and the structure it's attached to rattles. I reach up higher and find another rod—or, rung—to the ladder I'm pretty certain I've just discovered.

I climb up, trusting, hoping the next rung will be there as I reach, one at a time, up to an old wooden trapdoor, and I heave my shoulder into it. The hatch opens and light spills in, and I'm backstage at the Mercury.

A sunbeam slants through the hole in the roof above like a spotlight. The rest of the dome is in darkness. A pigeon passes through the light from outside and casts a long, bat-like shadow. It flaps into the heart of the dome and vanishes. Suddenly a chorus of flaps sets off, one after the other, fluttering in fury and echoing like the old theater is a bat cave.

I look around. There's no color anywhere. Just long shadows that ripple and breathe. Ash layers everything, gray and bumpy like I imagine the surface of the moon. I remember backstage, how it once was. The endless velvet curtains that hung. The spiderweb of ropes that were strung up on pulleys to the rafters, all of them gone. There's a set of old levers where a stagehand could, I guess, work the pulleys and traps that once made the show go on.

I make my way to center stage and look out at where the audience would be. The auditorium is stark and still as an old black-and-white photograph. Rows of seats line the walls all around like a cylinder up to the dome. They watch like frozen spectators—or *specters* . . . I wonder why those two words are so close. Is it because what ghosts really do is watch?

But I can hear something. Not sure what it is. Like the phantom of a thousand sounds that never died all the way out. Applause, overtures, whistles, shouts all pour down.

I see the seat in the front row where I sat the last time I ever saw my father.

I think of my father standing right here, and imagine what he looked out on before he vanished. The hundreds of astonished faces. His brothers. Mom. Me.

Something tells me to *turn around* and there's something that wasn't there before.

I think—*There's people behind me*—

But no. It's a mural on the back wall. My father and the Maestro are squared off in graphic, bright colors.

There's a strange backdrop. A dark landscape with mist

rolling over end-of-the-world cliffs. A branch of lightning splits clouds that billow in midstorm. Even the pitch-black empty spaces have depth, like I could step inside and walk there forever.

Pop is in his all-black suit, hands summoning light. I see myself in his face. There's my cheekbones, my dimple. I raise a hand, almost to say *Hi*.

My stomach grows cold when I look over at Maestro.

The magician's half-mirrored mask covers the left side of his otherwise plain face. Eyes like he's peering into a universe that's darker than the one we know.

I hate him.

It's his fault my dad's gone.

Pops disappeared going after Maestro. Vanished into the same Mirror before it shattered on the stage.

It was all set to be an amazing night. Magic Duel of the Century. I was there, in the audience, just eight years old. The memory feels new. Maybe not like it was yesterday but last week at the latest. The best and brightest of Echo City were there. Brooklyn glitz and style and swagger, all enchanted like.

But it went bad.

Pop—he owned the crowd with his routine. His floating light bulb trick. His vanishing, reappearing cards that no magician could ever figure out. That old creepy skull he had that let him read people's thoughts.

Then Maestro's turn. His assistant rolls out three large cabinets. Urma Tan, with eyes like frost and blond hair so pale it's almost white. Dressed in all black, with red fingernails long and curling like small serpents. They do Maestro's famous teleportation trick, where he would vanish Urma Tan from one cabinet to appear in another.

But then Maestro revealed his new trick. Urma Tan wheeled out the Mirror.

The Mirror was set in an elaborate carved-wood frame with a serpent eating its tail at the top, but the glass was what stood out to me. The surface didn't just reflect the world. It *was* another world, if that makes sense. The audience reflected in the Mirror was us, but wasn't us. It moved less like how a reflection moves and more like how a shadow moves, just a step behind its maker.

Maestro was looking into it like he was obsessed. Like he had forgotten all about the audience. Dad looked worried and I knew something was wrong.

Then Maestro walked toward the Mirror. Some energy was surging from within. A blue light appeared deep within the glass that grew and glimmered like a star.

Then Urma Tan dove into the Mirror.

You expected a crash, but she was gone. Just like that, without a sound.

It seemed like part of the act at first. The audience was impressed.

But Maestro looked devastated. Then he dove in right after her. Headfirst, like into a swimming pool. I braced myself for the crash, but again none came. He was just gone.

A beam of blue light flashed from the depths of the Mirror and shined somewhere backstage, behind the curtain. Sparks popped from the Mirror in every direction. The Mirror spat them out like sunflower seeds. They popped like exploding coal on the velvet curtains. The fire flared and spread.

And then, faster than I could think, like his mind had long been made up, Pop glanced to me and Mom with the faintest magical wink and jumped in after Maestro.

And he was gone, too.

Then the Mirror crashed to the floor in a thousand pieces.

I SLIDE MY feet along the dusty stage and think about the shards of glass. There's still black burn marks on the floor from the fire, but no glass. Not even glass dust. Someone must have come and swept it up. Maybe whoever painted that mural? Who would take the time to do something like that, paint a mural with so much care and detail where no one would ever see it?

And really, who would rearrange the letters on the marquee?

Wind gusts through the hole in the dome and swirls debris on center stage. The hairs along my arm tingle. I think about the Mirror and I make out the shape of a trapdoor on the stage floor. I clear the dust and ash with big sweeps of my feet. Magicians were famous for using these kinds of trapdoors in stages for all sorts of tricks. With this and the one I came down, the Mercury must be full of them. I give the stage a few stomps, then remember the levers backstage.

I jet over to them and pull every lever there—the up ones down, and the down ones up.

I hear the sound of old hinges grinding and the slap of the wooden hatch opening.

There, on center stage, the trapdoor hangs open.

I hustle over to it. Thinking, *What if it was all a trick? Like Black Herman's burial?*

What if he's just . . . been down there all these years?

Just as I'm starting to worry about how he's been eating, and am wondering if he's starving or a skeleton or what, I peer down into the open hatch.

The sunbeam from the hole in the roof has a pink-orange glow. It hits just the right spot to light up the chamber below. There's an old Houdini-style trunk, like the ones he used to chain himself up in and pop out of moments later.

I hop down and barely feel the impact on my feet.

Sure, the chest is a little small for a whole person, but Dad is a great magician and could fold himself up and I'm sure he's fine in there . . .

I knock on the old wood and say, "Dad? Dad? It's me." I try not to be distracted by how I don't hear anything in response or by thoughts of how anyone could actually be alive after all these years. I just focus on *how to get this old thing open.*

There are chains wrapped around the trunk and an old padlock. The chains are just for show, I'm sure—the lock is the key to getting the thing open. The padlock has four rotating rings of digits, requiring a four-digit code. Then I see, carved into the wall above the chest, some familiar letters:

Ybbx Sbejneq naq Onpxjneq, Vg'f Nyy gur Fnzr

The same letters from the Watch of 13 plaque in Long Fingers's workshop. *Look forward and backward, it's all the same.*

Forward and backward, it's all the same . . .

My fingers trembling, knowing this *has* to be a message *meant for me*, knowing what the numbers are as I flick the padlock to 1 . . . 3 . . . 1 . . . 3 . . .

Forward and backward, it's all the same.

The numbers that you count forward and backward on the Watch of 13 are . . .

13, 13!

The padlock clicks open. My hands are a blur as I strip the chains from around the chest, open it up, thinking, *Pop, I'm coming, Pop!*

But there's no person inside the trunk.

When I come to my senses, I am relieved he's not actually in there. I mean, he would be a four-year-old skeleton if he were.

There's just one small thing at the bottom of the trunk.

It's a box.

Just a box.

It *is* a nice box.

Mahogany, well made. Each side has a carving on it. A deck of cards on one, a pistol on another, a skull on the third side, and a square on the fourth. The designs are elaborate, with swirls and flourishes like the box was made way back in the day. But unlike this old theater, the box hasn't aged at all. There's no dust, no scratches, no nicks, or any damage at all. I try to open it but there's no give. The thing feels solid as a log.

I don't know how long I spend turning the box over, examining it, prodding it, and thinking about how to get in. There's a complicated brass piece connecting the top of the box to the body, and it looks like some kind of locking mechanism. There's a circular opening that reveals layers of gears within, like the inside of a clock.

After a quick hesitation, I rotate the top and it moves real smooth, like somebody just hit it with WD-40. As the hole in the top of the box turns, the gears on the inside follow, and those curved brass bars oscillate around and around until the segments all align to form another circle just within the box. A number is revealed in brass in the recesses of the gears that you couldn't see before: 13. I judge the size of the circle that the curved brass bars just formed and . . .

Could it be?

I take the pocket watch out from around my neck and set it in the circle, just over the brass number 13. It fits like the last piece of a jigsaw puzzle.

There's a *click* as the lock releases and the clock hands start moving. The lid of the box parts like lips about to whisper.

Pop, I think. *You wanted me to find this.*

OR DID HE, *though?*

My blood is pounding, like I can feel my pulse with each tick of the clock hand running the circle of numbers, all the way into my fingertips as I raise the lid of the box.

I warn myself not to get carried away.

Maybe other people know about the Watch of 13.

Long Fingers knows.

Others must know.

But another voice says, *This is a message from Dad, he's reaching out to me, from wherever he is, like I always knew he would—*

Then I snap out of it as what's in the box comes into focus.

There's a sheet of paper, but not like you'd see at school. It looks old, like something in a museum.

And it's floating.

Right in the center of the box, hovering like a hummingbird in midair.

I'm looking for the strings, the magnets, the part that would explain *how this is possible*, but there's just this levitating piece of folded-up paper.

I'm scared to touch it. What if it's some kind of trap? Who knows who's been here since my dad disappeared?

I try to slow my thoughts and take in my surroundings. It's a small space, the sort of spot a magician might hide in after they've disappeared onstage. The box isn't hidden behind some fake wall or bookcase. It's right here in the open. How has nobody found this thing? Or maybe they have, and I'm just the first one to figure out how to open it?

The first one to come here with this Watch of 13.

So maybe, I think, *whatever is in this box* is *meant for me.*

And I wonder what the paper says. I *have* to see what's on it.

I snatch the page out lightning quick, and then wait a moment with my eyes shut for spikes to fly from the wall or a giant boulder to crush me from above.

When nothing happens, I open the paper to reveal a map.

Looks like a map of Echo City, drawn by hand.

Just a map.

No Xs marking any spots.

I reach my hand back into the box. I feel around the felt-lined bottom and corners for vents or magnets or strings or something to explain the hovering map, and I hear—

"*Yooo—*"

And somebody crashes into me.

A sudden blue light flashes from the box and fills the trap like a light bulb popping.

My face hits the floor. The light hurts my eyes. The box is stuck underneath me. I feel like I just took a clown-size shoe to the back. There is a body on top of me. So much body it can really only be one person.

"King?" Too Tall says, relieved to see it's me. "Wha— what happened? I'm sorry, my dude, you okay?"

Too Tall's words sound distant. The wind is knocked out of me. It takes a few breaths for everything to come back into focus. I try to push myself up, but my left hand is *stuck in the box.*

How is that even possible?

Too Tall is saying, "Am I glad to see you! We went down that chute after you and next thing I know, I'm totally lost and alone. No you, no Veronica. Wandering around, like, man, this place gives me the creeps. And then—I see this mural, I'm backtracking and *wham* I fall down a hole in the stage! But you already knew that. Need a hand?"

Too Tall is on his feet in a crouch, offering to help me up.

I yank my hand from the box to take his—

—and it's gone—

Too Tall's mouth opens but he doesn't make a sound.

My left hand is gone.

There is nothing there.

There's no stump. No bones. No blood. Just no hand. There's a faint blue glow where my wrist ends and the rest of my hand has vanished, like it's been erased. It's like those Bunsen burners from science class, just a blue vapor and then nothing.

But I can still feel my hand.

Can't I?

I hold it up to my face but I just see Too Tall, jaw hanging on for dear life.

"Th-th-there's no . . ." His words come out at half the speed as normal.

"*Shh,*" I say, holding a finger to my lips. I realize I can actually feel my finger against my lips.

I can't see my hand, but I can feel it?

"*Shh*?" Tall repeats. "Why *shhh*? You don't have a hand and you're worried about me talking?"

"Sorry! I just didn't want to hear the words *don't have a hand.*"

"What else is there to say right now? What other words of all the words would I say? You don't have a hand!"

"I—I—" I close my eyes.

Calm. Breathe.

Just because Tall is saying I don't have a hand and I don't exactly *see* a hand at the end of my wrist doesn't mean I don't have a hand. Maybe if I open my eyes, I *will* see my hand, and Too Tall and I were just hilariously mistaken . . .

I open my eyes. No dice. No hand. No hand at all.

Then I realize—Too Tall is by himself.

"Wait—where's Veronica?"

"I don't know, dude, I was saying before. We all got separated at the chute."

"You think she's okay?" I ask.

"Dude—is *she* okay? Are *you* okay?"

"Am I?"

Am I okay? I repeat in my head. And then again, *Am I okay? Am I?*

"I don't know, Tall. This is beyond insane." I stare at the empty space that my hand used to occupy.

"Bananas," he says. "King. What happened?"

I catch my breath and tell him about the chest all chained up, about the code and the box.

"This box here," I say, and reach for it on the floor. First with my right hand. Then I decide to try to pick it up with my left, my ghosted hand. I grab the box and the sensation of my fingers is there. Thumb, pointer, pinkie, and the others—I can feel them all. The wood is smooth and dense and the metal of the Watch of 13 lodged in the lock is cool.

I glance over at Too Tall and realize by his horrified look that to him the box appears to be floating in the air by the end of my wrist.

"H-how are you doing that?" he asks, spooked out of his mind.

"I—I don't know. I mean, I'm just holding it. But I can't see my hand. I can feel it—I just can't see it."

"That makes two of us."

I offer the box to Tall. He hesitates to take it.

"What?" I ask.

"I don't know. That box cost you your hand," he says, taking a step back into a corner of grime. "So you found a strange box in an abandoned theater and thought, hey, let me just shove my hand in there?"

"It's not just some strange box. Well, maybe it is, but Tall, I'm thinking my dad wanted me to find this box. I mean, it was the watch he left me that opened it."

"Your dad," says Tall. "The one that disappeared?"

"Yeah . . ."

"That vanished? Ghosted? Went and got *gone*?"

"Yeah," I say, my voice shrinking.

What if the rest of me disappears, too? What if the hand is just the beginning? What if this is what happened to Pops?

In all my fantasies of coming to the Mercury, of reliving that night Pops disappeared, it's always me who stops Pop from vanishing. *I'm* the one who brings *him* back. Never, not once, did I disappear, too.

But Pop vanished and *so could I.*

"Stay with me, King," Too Tall says.

"I—I'm trying, but what if I can't help it? What if I go, too?"

"Don't talk like that. You feel strange? You feel, I don't know, vanish-y?"

"I don't know. I don't know what that feels like. I want my hand back. I'd feel better with my hand back."

"I hear you. But the rest of you. Still here, yeah?"

I put my hand to my face—lips, eyes, cheeks—then the rest of me. Neck. Elbows. Chest. Everything checks out. My heart, beating like a jackhammer. My tummy, turning with the grease from the pizza.

"Everything else's where it's supposed to be," I say.

Tall takes my wrist, braves the weirdness of it, and plants his very visible palm into my vanished one. Our palms collide with a *pop*. His fingers collapse around my phantom knuckles. He's gripping my hand—but we can only see his, alone, like a pantomime handshake.

"You still here, King," he says, "you still here all right."

NEW VOICES CRASH into the theater. They hoot and echo in chaos and I can't make out what they're saying. The theater suddenly sounds like a playground at recess. Could be anywhere from six to twenty noisy kids running down the aisles.

Too Tall's eyes go wide, like, *What now?*

Then a thin, commanding voice slices through the noise above like a razor blade.

"Spread out," it says. "Find them."

And just those words ghost all that ruckus. Footsteps rush down the aisles toward the stage.

I wonder, *Did they get in through the front doors?*

Or the chute?

And I remember that I left the code written out on the sidewalk in chalk. Could they have figured out how to read the code and found the brick wall?

I turn to Too Tall in panic. I open my mouth to say something about the code but he puts a finger to his lips.

I nod and keep quiet as a church mouse.

But I look at the sunbeam from above that spotlights center stage and realize it won't matter. This trap will be the first place they look.

And I remember those white magician's gloves that Crooked Eye gave me.

I take them out of my backpack and slide one on my ghosted hand. I worry again for a moment that the hand is really gone, but the glove fits right over it and you'd never know . . .

What? That you don't have but sorta still have a hand? That Ma is going to be like, "King, I know I gave birth to a kid with two hands. Now what in god's name have you done with the other one?"

I tell myself to breathe.

To *calm down*.

And after a couple deep breaths I think, *How did*

these kids just happen to show up now? I get a bad feeling that this is no coincidence. They could have been hiding nearby, waiting for me to find this box. They could even know I have the Watch of 13. The timing is too close together. So I slip the box into my backpack and strap it on my shoulders.

"Uh-oh, King," says Tall.

There's a kid sitting in the open trapdoor with his legs dangling above us. He has a pair of intense green eyes, and he looks *rough*.

There's a scar etched across his neck like a barbed-wire choke collar. He's a little older than me, definitely a teenager, but beyond that I couldn't tell his age. Maybe it's the strange lighting, or the dust and ash surrounding us, but his face is this gray color that looks barely human. There are scars on his cheeks, scribbled symbols like doodles you sketch in the margins of your math textbook. His pupils are tiny pinpricks in the bright meadow green of his eyes. He smiles like a creature that doesn't smile but has heard about smiles.

He holds out a hand. His boys gather around. They all have that strange ash-gray color to their skin, like you can't even tell if they're black or white or what.

"Give me the Lost and Found," he orders.

I'm speechless. I don't even know what he's talking

about. *Does he want the box? Did he see me put it in my backpack?* I can't say for sure.

"Get outta here, Mint," says Too Tall. He tries to puff up his chest but his voice is shaky. "How about *you* get lost . . . and found."

Mint makes a *tried-this-the-easy-way* face and simply says, "Smoke them out."

I hear the flick of a light and something metal lands in our chamber and bounces around, hissing. Too Tall and I watch as two cola cans with lit fuses roll to a stop on the floor between us, spitting out sparks like makeshift smoke bombs.

"Who walks around with *smoke bombs*?" Tall shrieks before covering his face with his fitted cap.

The cans unleash clouds of smoke that flood the trap. I try to cover up, but smoke streams through my fingers and eyelids, tears stinging my face. I squeeze my eyes shut in blinding pain.

"We got to get outta here!" Tall coughs.

"Now come up," I hear Mint's voice. "Or I'll shut this trap and let you two steam like a couple lobsters."

"Okay," says Tall. "You win, let us out!"

I hate to admit it, but he's right. We're helpless down here, both of us.

"Take my hand," Mint says as I blindly reach up for it. "Closer," he says, "closer," until I feel his stiff grip. He pulls me up and out of the trap. As soon as I get back onstage, his boys grab me and pin my arms behind my back.

"Give me the box," orders Mint.

"Too Tall"—I cough—"get him out." I can barely open my eyes. The sting is still so sharp.

"Yo, Mint!" I hear Tall shout from below the stage. "Come on, man!"

I squint to see smoke billowing from the trapdoor behind Mint as he glares like a demon. His faceless crew tightens their grip on me.

"I'll make you a deal," says Mint. "Give me the box and I'll help your friend."

"Help him out now!" I say. If I just hand over the box, how do I know he'll do what he says?

"What, help him out of here?" Mint says with a nasty snicker.

My vision clears up just enough to watch him reach down into the smoke and pull the trapdoor closed with a *thud*.

"No!" I shout.

Too Tall hollers from under the stage, hoarse and desperate. There's snickers and laughter from all around. I lunge at Mint but his minions hold me back. My blood goes hot. I pull and yank and claw in rage.

Suddenly, the trapdoor opens again and smoke shoots up and Too Tall shouts with relief. "Whoa, that's better! Now get me outta here!"

Mint looks confused by the door having opened.

Who did that? Somebody must have worked the backstage levers. *Veronica?* I wonder.

"Give me that bag," Mint snaps, and grabs my backpack strap and yanks hard. I hook my arm to it and hold on for dear life, hold on with everything, thinking, *This box is mine, my dad wanted me to have this—*

And I feel this strange energy suddenly course through my hand—the ghosted hand—almost like it's heating up like a kettle until it reaches a point where the hand can't contain all that hot anymore and I swing it at Mint and—

I look up to see all the smoke, every curling, steaming inch of it, has gathered beneath the roof into the shape of a giant fist. A smoke-made fist the size of a wrecking ball. My fist and the smoke fist both speed toward Mint and—

—boom—

The bag goes slack. No one is pulling on it anymore.

I open my eyes. I can see again.

The smoke fist is gone, now the stage is covered in fog, and there's a large puff of smoke coming from the stage trap. Completely normal and not at all in the shape of a giant fist.

All those bodies that were surrounding me are gone.

Mint is gone.

Then I realize they aren't *gone* gone. Not *Dad* gone. They've just moved a ways back.

Mint has fallen clean off the stage and is spread out somewhere between the third- and fourth-row orchestra seats. Like about ten to fifteen feet away.

The rest of his crew isn't far from him. They were all blasted off the stage. They writhe around the seats and aisles, dazed but awake. I'm standing center stage, alone.

"Tall!" I rush to the trapdoor. "Tall!" I shout down into the thick layers of smoke. I can barely make out his shape through the gray curtain.

"Yo, King!" I'm relieved to hear his voice—at least he sounds with-it. "What in the world is going on up there?" He coughs.

"You okay, man? I'm getting you out!" I say. I drop to my knees and reach my gloved hand into the trap. "Come toward me!"

And as soon as I speak, I feel Too Tall's hand collide

with mine. "Whoa!" he says, like he's as surprised as I am. I brace myself to pull him up, but I'm amazed by how easy it is—he practically floats up the chamber by the tug of my hand, and then he's beside me onstage.

He's still holding his hat over his face. When he removes it, his eyes are red and teary, but he looks okay.

"How—did you do that?" he asks.

"I—I don't really know. I don't know how I did any of it. You good, Tall?" I ask.

"Yeah, I think so," he says, staring at my gloved hand.

I follow his gaze. The white glove is lit up with a faint blue glow like a colored light bulb with fingers.

"My man, how are you doing that?"

"I don't know!"

"And look at this," he says, and shows me a clear crystal about the size of a dinner knife.

"What's that?" I ask.

"No clue. I slipped on it down there when the smoke was everywhere."

"That thing was just down there? I swear it wasn't there before," I say, and examine the crystal. It reflects the blue glow from my hand. My hand . . .

"Did you see the fist?" I ask him. "The fist made of smoke?"

"What smoke fist?"

Before I can answer, a voice shouts from behind me, "King, come on, let's go!"

And I remember how the trapdoor opened. Like someone had worked the lever backstage . . .

It's Veronica. She's all the way stage left, pointing, and it seems like she knows what she's saying and where she's going.

I wonder how long she's been waiting and watching, and I am *so* glad to see her.

WE FOLLOW VERONICA to a set of stairs that leads us one level down, and then to another trap that leads to a ladder. The ladder leads us to the sewers.

"V—you knew this was here?" I ask, descending the metal rungs.

"The chute from out front. It led me here," she says. "I climbed back up this way to get to the theater."

I touch my foot to a long tunnel made of dark, wet bricks.

"Make sure you shut that door!" she calls to Too Tall.

There are two walking platforms, one on either side of the running filth and sludge.

"Come on," says V. "They'll try to follow. Look alive."

She's moving fast, ducking past rusty pipes. I hurry after her. She's found another ladder on the side of the tunnel. Veronica climbs without a word. It's even darker up the ladder than it is in the tunnel.

"Can you guys help me?" she calls. "This manhole cover is too heavy."

She comes back down and Too Tall quickly climbs up and starts pushing and forcing the underside of the manhole cover, but the thing is really heavy. As I watch Tall struggle, I think about what's just happened. I hold my hand up and watch it ripple with blue light beneath the glove. *I moved all those boys. I made a fist out of smoke,* I think, *and then I moved Too Tall. I put him back onstage like it was nothing. With this.*

"Tall," I say, "let me try something."

I wave my hand at the manhole and concentrate like I'm trying to push, like the round iron lid is right there in my hand.

It opens. Streetlight suddenly beams into the shaft. Too Tall slides the cover along the sidewalk with a scrape and we're free.

The street is quiet as we step into an alley. Folks walk by on the avenue like it's just another ordinary evening in ordinary ole Echo City.

Veronica grabs me by the shoulders and spins me around to look at her.

"Now, what in the world was that?"

"I—uh, um . . ."

Where do I even start?

"His hand," says Too Tall, giving me up. "His hand, like, disappeared but it's still there actually and it's just pure magic or something. And I think it kinda moved that manhole cover, 'cause it was too heavy for me."

I give Tall a long stare.

He shrugs. Then elbows me. "What, you think you're gonna figure this out on your own? Show her!"

He may have a point.

"Yeah, King, show me." Veronica's eyes are tired and her hair is mussed up. There's a little pulse popping behind her jaw that I've only seen when she's really worried about something.

I pull the glove off my hand.

"To be honest," I say, "there's not a lot to see."

She gets the point. She puts her fingers to her astonished lips.

"And you're saying your hand is still there somehow?" she asks.

I reach to touch her. She flinches at first, just like Too

Tall did, then relaxes as I take her hand in mine. I feel her warm flesh, clammy with sweat. "See? Still there."

"I see," she says, squeezing my hand as she stares at her own hand gripped around nothing. "Or I don't see. I mean, I get . . . I mean, *wow*."

"Can I ask you, V? How long were you watching us?"

"Long enough," she says.

I ask, "Long enough to see the smoke form the shape of a fist?"

She looks at me like I'm nuts. "It's not exactly something you miss," she says.

"*I* missed it!" Tall whips his head back to V. "*You* saw it?"

"How did you *do* that?" she grills me, like she's more worried than impressed.

I think: *How did I do that?*

"Those guys were all over me. I mean, I was surrounded, Mint had my backpack, I could barely see anything, I was upset about how they trapped Too Tall, and then—my hand—well, you saw. You tell me. What did it look like?"

"It was like . . . all the smoke suddenly woke up and changed direction and gathered up into a giant fist, like a smoke ring, but with knuckles."

"*Wow*," says Too Tall.

"Yeah," I say. "That's what I saw, too. Tell me, you think it looked like, I dunno, *my* hand?"

"I don't know, King! Maybe? Who notices how a giant smoke hand looks?"

"I'm just wondering, that's all."

"Well, you're messing with some scary stuff. Powerful stuff. It wasn't just the smoke hand, King—that wasn't the scariest part. It crashed down like your fist was *controlling the smoke fist.* Your left hand was glowing blue and that fist and the smoke fist synchronized and *wham.* There was this *blast.* Those boys went flying, I bet you broke some bones. Mint—I mean, he *flew.* It was . . . the craziest thing I've ever seen," she says like she never expected to say that phrase and actually mean it.

I glance at Too Tall. He can't stop tapping his giant feet. I can't tell if he's nervous or excited. "You saved me, though," he says, and takes my hand and holds it fast, like he means it. "I won't forget that. Not ever."

"Thank Veronica, too," I say. "She's the one that opened the trapdoor when Mint closed it on you, so you could breathe."

"You did that for me?" Tall says, touching a closed fist over his heart. "Thank you, V. They could have caught you backstage. You didn't have to do that."

"Don't mention it," she says, like she's a little uncomfortable with the attention. "Mint is just terrible. I don't understand what happened to him. He didn't use to be like that."

"I know. He even looks different," says Tall. "All of those boys do. Like they're, I don't know, what's the reverse of a suntan? Anyway, we better get moving. Don't want to see them again."

But Veronica has her attention back on my hand. "How did this happen?" she asks me.

I tell her about the trunk beneath the stage, how I opened the lock and found this strange box, and how Too Tall fell on me and my hand went *through* the box somehow, and there was a blast of light from the box, and how Tall found that crystal down there after that . . .

"That kid with the green eyes—he called this box the 'Lost and Found' or something," I say. "They came into the theater for it, I think."

"But you still have it?"

"Yeah." I put my glove back on and take the box out for her to see.

She examines the pocket watch still lodged in the locking mechanism. "Wow. Your dad's watch . . ."

"Look. It's running now. It's never worked before, but

once I put the watch in the lock, the hands started moving."

She thinks this over but says nothing. Traffic passes by on the street outside the alley. It's getting late.

"And there's a map inside," I say.

She opens the box and looks at the map. "It's Echo City," she says.

"V, you know why those kids would want that box? Or is it the map they want? You think they knew I got it open somehow?"

"I don't know, King. I really don't. Mint and those kids—they hang around that weird house on Torrini."

"Where the She-Wizard of Torrini Boulevard lives?" says Too Tall, and makes the sign of the cross.

"I guess?" says Veronica. "They're into some weird cult stuff, daring each other to jump off buildings and break police car windows, crazy as a bag of cats. They're the type of kids that pull the legs off a spider 'cause they're bored. I stay away from them. You should, too," she warns.

"Gladly. But what if they come looking for me? I mean, they know I've got the box and I'm not exactly hard to find."

She sighs. "Jeez, King. You've been in town less than forty-eight hours and already stirred the hornets' nest. I mean, these guys can *sting*. I hate to say it, but you need help. You've got to tell someone."

"Tell my mom? That we broke into the Mercury? She'd flip!"

She closes her eyes like she's going to regret what she's about to say. "I was actually thinking of . . . *my* parent."

VERONICA LEADS THE way to the old bookcase wall.

She's spent the last twenty minutes preparing Uncle Long Fingers for my hand situation. I spent that time being cross-examined by Mom about why we got home at 9:00 p.m. instead of 8:00. I told her about meeting Eddie "Too Tall" at Not Not Ray's. She remembered him. I said we lost track of time, hanging out. I think she bought it, but you never know. I'm actually surprised we were only an hour late.

When Ma and Crooked start cleaning the kitchen from dinner, Veronica gives me the sign. I stand beside her as she pulls the book to open the secret door.

Then she lets me go in ahead of her.

"You're not coming?"

"Listen, thanks to tonight, I have now entered that old, musty lab exactly 1.5 times, and that's 1.5 times too many. Find me when you're done. And good luck."

My uncle is exactly how he was the first time I came in here. Same ratty beard, same fried eyes, same tired expression, and I'm pretty sure he's working on the same trick or device or whatever beneath that massive tarp.

"Hey, Unc," I say.

He holds out one of those long hands he's known for. "Lemme see the box."

I give it over.

For some reason, it feels like a teacher grading my paper in red ink right in front of the whole class. He examines the box for what feels like forever. Taps it, knocks it, opens it, right side up, upside down.

As he works, I can't help but wonder, *Did he leave it there under the stage for me to find?* I know it sounds out-there, but there's only so many people who could have known the code and put it up on the marquee—my pops, and him . . . But if he did, then all this box examining is a bunch of playacting, and Uncle Long Fingers just doesn't seem the sort to mess with all of that. No, if Uncle Long had wanted me to have that box, he'd probably just have walked into my bedroom and dropped it on me and left without a word.

He sets the box down on his desk and places his hand on top.

"Well, congratulations," he says in a dry tone. "You found Preston's old box. The Magician's Lost and Found. One hundred percent authentic, not a fake or a copy." He lets out a sigh. "Now tell me how you found it."

I tell him. I don't leave anything out, at least not deliberately. I tell him about the code, the watch, and the moment I found it—

"That's when the hand . . . *happened*?" he asks.

Knew he'd get to that.

"Yeah," I say.

He holds out his hand toward me just like he had for the box.

As I give him my gloved hand, I realize that he needs to touch things to understand them. Probably how he got his nickname.

Without a word, he rolls my white magician's glove up onto my fingertips so it looks like the glove is floating like a marshmallow without the stick.

Now, I'm *still* startled to see that there's nothing there, but for whatever reason, Long Fingers isn't. He just looks like a scientist observing science stuff. He then takes my glove all the way off and holds my wrist by the faint blue glow up to his work light.

Which is about the same as just, well, looking directly at the light.

Then he gives it back to me, and hands me back the glove, and asks me to explain everything, and he means *everything*, that happened.

And I do.

And he asks me to repeat the whole story, including everything, and he means *everything* . . .

And I repeat the story and try not to skip anything.

Then he asks me to focus on the part when Too Tall fell on me. When my hand went through the box.

"There was a flash of light?" he asks.

"Yeah."

"What color was it?"

"Blue light," I say.

He nods, sighs, and leans back, clearly bothered by something.

"Your uncle—my brother, as it were—Crooked Eye believes that children shouldn't know any more than they can handle. My question is, how does anyone know what they can handle until it's there to be handled? Child or no. Kids are adaptable, isn't that right, li'l King?"

"Sure."

"So I'll put it to you plainly. Your father ain't exactly gone. But he ain't never coming back."

I wasn't expecting that. I was expecting something about the box or my *invisible hand . . .*

Uncle Long goes on. "I see you're quiet for once. Good. That's wise. 'Cause there's a lot to open your mind to, and if you're busy talking or thinking up questions or what to say, you also busy not listening."

"I'm listening," I blurt.

He pauses and looks at me cross, like I'm not getting his point. "Well, what'd I just say?"

"Your father ain't exactly gone. But he ain't never coming back," I repeat.

"Well, yeah. Now you remember yesterday—what you first came in my lab here to ask me?"

"I thought you said not to think up questions—"

"Quit trying so hard to be smart, kid, you'll get a brain cramp," he snaps.

He's right. He's here trying to tell me something important. It's almost like I can't help it. Like, if I sit here and listen to what he has to tell me, I won't be a kid anymore.

"Okay. I came to ask . . ." What did I ask? About where's Pop? About why we don't magic the dishes clean every night? What was it? "I asked about real magic."

"That's right, you did. And to be honest, that impressed me. Because it's the first and most important question, out of all the stuff that your mama don't want you to know and Crooked don't want you to know. Something, I think, your daddy was close to wanting to tell you when you got a little older."

"That—?"

"That yes. Magic is real. Really real."

I nod and blink a few times. Now I already know that magic is really real, but it's still startling to hear an adult actually admit something.

"And what's happening with my hand?" I ask. "I know it's magic. But, like, do you get what's going on?"

"I'm getting to that. But it starts with your daddy, and where he's gone, and why he had to go."

"Why did he?" I ask.

"He was protecting us."

"Couldn't he protect us *and* stay? Did he have to *go*?"

My uncle's eyelids seem heavy, but I think he's more sad than sleepy. He slumps his shoulders.

"I've asked myself that question maybe a thousand times," he says. "And a thousand times, the answer is yes. He had to go."

"But why?"

"Here's where you got to understand how the whole magic thing works. Now, you've been to the aquarium, yes?"

"Which one?"

He sighs. "You've been to *an* aquarium?"

"Yes."

"Okay, you know how you're on one side, and there's this thick glass, and on the other side of the glass it's all water and aquatic life, yeah?"

"Yeah."

"That's how our world is with magic. We're protected by something like that thick glass, though you can't see it. And on the other side of that glass is magic, or a magical realm. Some folks call it the Realm. Now, say there was a fish, ended up on our side of the glass. Just to survive, they would need some of that water. Just to survive, they would be letting some of the Realm into our world. That's like cracking a hole in that glass between you and the fishes and whatnot on the other side of the aquarium, you get me?"

"I think I do. So there's a fish from the other side of the glass. And it's drawing water into our reality?"

"Exactly. Now, when glass gets too many cracks in it, what happens to it?"

I close my eyes, and think of the Mirror onstage at the Mercury. "It shatters."

"Exactly. Reality itself would explode. So Maestro's Mirror? That thing was like a hole clean through the glass. A portal that allowed Maestro to jump into the Realm. Only something was pulling the Realm into our world, too, and if Preston hadn't destroyed it?" He slowly shakes his head and draws an imaginary line across his throat. "That's all she wrote."

"But what's that mean? What would happen? Like, how could it be so bad?"

He gives me a look that's serious as a graveyard. "What happens when the glass breaks at the aquarium?"

"I'm guessing your feet get wet."

"Well, imagine all the water in the ocean is on the other side. No end to it gushing all around you, up to your ears, until the reality on the other side of that glass drowns our reality as we know it. No breathing, no thinking, no anything. Us and everything we know, gone. Replaced by whatever comes through that busted glass." He shakes his head. "Your pop saved us all."

"So why couldn't Dad have just broken the Mirror? Why did he have to jump through?"

"Here's the kicker. If he'd broken the Mirror from *our* side of things, that portal? It would remain open in *perpetuity*." He draws the word out like it has a dozen syllables. Then he pauses to make sure I understand. "No, Preston had to shatter the portal from *inside the Realm*. That was the only way to close it."

"So what's all this got to do with this box?"

"A little device of Preston's. He was always looking for a safe way to access the Realm without making a rift. When you put your hand in there, and your buddy Too Tall fell on you, you must have made a rift anyways. What with the blue light and all of that. A small rift, but a rift between worlds nonetheless. Your hand must have got stuck in the in-between. I never heard of anything like that happening. But that's the only explanation I got for your hand there, doing what it's doing."

"It's not doing a whole lot," I grumble.

"Doing a lot more than you know, being in two places at once. Part of your hand is here, in our world. That's how you can put your glove on and climb ladders and alla that. But part of your hand is *there*. In the *Realm*. And that's how you conjured a smoke fist and sent those kids flying a couple football fields."

I stare at my gloved hand, tapping each finger to my thumb. "Are you saying I can *touch* the Realm, somehow?"

"It sounds like you already did."

"So if I can touch the Realm, and Pop is *in* the Realm, can't I, like, touch him?"

"Listen, King, it's very important that you *don't try to use your hand to touch the Realm*. Remember that fish out of water I was talking about? Imagine it's more like a shark. And you're just chum. Whatever Realm power you tap into, she'll smell it like blood in the water. You copy that?"

"I copy," I repeat, though it's only a reflex. "But who is this shark you're talking about? Why'd you call her 'she'?"

For the first time since I've been down here, Long Fingers perks up. He hefts his large, lumbering body out of that chair with the grace of a forklift and walks around his worktable and over to me. He squares me up by the shoulders, then puts his hands on his knees to bend to my eye level. His eyes are little brown cocoa beans in shot glasses of milk.

"Do. Not. Try. To. Use. Your. Hand. Don't think about what it can do, and don't try and find out. I want you to leave this box with me, and I'll work on a way to get you right again. In the meantime, keep cool, wear that glove, and don't tell anyone about this. Bad enough my daughter knows, li'l Princess of Mischief, that one." He scrunches his mouth like this next bit is difficult to chew. "Now, I'd never tell you to hide anything from your ma . . ."

"But you're telling me to do that?"

"I said I'd *never* do that. You know y'all's relationship better than I do, and if you think she can hand—"

"I won't say a word, Unc."

He holds his hands up. "Your call. But listen, if you try and use that hand, and the Realm starts leaking in, and I find out, and I *will* find out, I'll smell it—I'ma have to tell her. Because it's too important. And if you won't listen to me, you for sure better listen to her."

"I won't use it. I promise."

"You sure?"

"Yeah. If we lost Pop because this Realm stuff is that

important, that's enough for me," I say, but I feel like I'm trying out the words to see how they sound. "I got one question, though. Couldn't we use, like, just enough magic to bring Dad back? And then that's it?"

He turns around and holds a pain in his lower back. "Good night, Young King. Good. Night."

I'M SITTING OUTSIDE on the stoop and I can't imagine hitting the pillow. I am wired, my heart racing like it's got enough voltage running through it to power the county grid.

At 4:00 a.m., the street is so quiet I'd believe I'm back in the suburbs. Must be how they grow trees in Brooklyn, extra thick and gnarly and lush. The leaves swish in the breeze like they're whispering secrets.

The one word that keeps playing in my head, from all the info my uncle just dumped on me, is *sacrifice* . . .

Because that's what I understand now that maybe I never understood before.

I always had a sense that Pop did what he did for the

greater good, because that's the kind of person he is . . . or *was*? *Is*? I'm still not even sure.

And when I think about my hand, and the power that's somehow at my invisible fingertips, and how I conjured a blast that scattered a handful of punks like bowling pins, the one thought that keeps me from tempting that power now is *sacrifice*.

If I lost Dad because he made a sacrifice, then I have to . . .

Also sacrifice.

I take my glove off to see if there's been any change. But nothing.

Nothing at all.

Part of my hand, I guess the part I can't see, is in the Realm . . .

And Dad is in the Realm.

Doesn't that mean I could touch him?

The door opens behind me and the light casts two silhouettes down the stoop, mine and Veronica's.

"Whatup, cuzzo."

I put the white glove back on.

Veronica sits on the top step beside me, gives my face a good once-over, and smirks. "You look like how I feel after talking to my father for an hour."

I chuckle and force a smile, but I'm just being polite.

"*Oof.* That bad, huh? Well, sorry to interrupt. I can see you're staring out at the tree-lined block all romantic and pensive and whatnot." She puts a hand on my shoulder like she's about to get up. "Happy soul searching!"

"Wait," I say. "Stay, please. Just got a lot on my mind, is all."

"I know it, I do."

"How much do you know?"

"You mean, like, about *the Realm*?" she says in a mock-spooky voice that actually does make me laugh for real.

"So you do know."

"Only because I, like, spy on my dad and my uncle sometimes. Made my dad come clean one time, last May. He told me your dad jumped into that Mirror to save, like, reality itself or something. Pretty cool." She shrugs. "Cooler than anything my dad ever did."

"V, that doesn't exactly make me feel better."

"Well, maybe you're looking at this the wrong way? I mean, sure, you lost your father. But he didn't abandon you. I mean, he had a *purpose.* That's kinda noble, don't you think? It's rare enough that people do anything good for anyone, much less for *every*one. You know, King? People are terrible. But your father, he's, like, not at all terrible."

"Wow. You've got some low expectations, huh?"

"Can you blame me? My ma gave me up to that cantankerous blob back there. No one even told me why, but I know it wasn't 'cause she was trying to save the world or anything. King, she was my *mother* and she gave me up. Like, if your mother doesn't have your back, who does?"

I see a different side of Veronica then. She looks angry. And sure, I've seen lots of versions of her being angry, but usually she wears this smirk like she knows she's got one up on all the suckers of the world. Now she looks like the opposite. Like she's missing this one piece of basic equipment that everyone else walks around with, and it's so natural that people like me don't even realize we've got it. *A mother to love you.* Wow. That's like missing a lung.

"Now, don't go feeling sorry for me or nothing like that," she warns me, maybe reading my expression. "I don't want that at all. I will leave your little mopey self out here right now," she digs at me, but her smile is gentle.

"Nah, I get it, V. Sometimes it feels like the stuff that happens to me is all that matters. But everybody goes through stuff. Is it weird, though, that, after all this talk about how noble my dad was or is or whatever, all this about how I should appreciate what he did for the greater good, it just makes me want him back, like, even more?"

"Yeah, I feel you. I mean, what can ya do?" she says, shrugging.

I feel something then, in my gloved hand. A tingling pressure that gets more and more insistent. Almost like fingertips pressing into my flesh.

"What is it?" asks Veronica.

"I—I don't know."

I take off the glove. I almost expect to see thumbs digging into my palm. But there's nothing there, of course.

Then something very different presses into my hand. A crunch, like paper, like a balled-up piece of paper tucked into my palm, and then the other pressure closes my invisible fingers around the ball.

"King, what is it? You look like you're seeing a ghost."

I'm speechless. I feel my fist clutching onto a ball of paper, but I see absolutely nothing.

Then the pressure is gone. Nothing holding my fist closed.

So I open up my hand.

Out drops a balled-up sheet of yellow legal paper.

It lands between me and Veronica on the top step.

"Okay, wow. Where did that come from?" Veronica looks up. "There a large paper pigeon above us?"

I stare at the yellow ball and put my glove back on. I'm thinking I shouldn't take it off anymore. Strange things seem to happen when I do.

"It was like someone crumpled it up and put it in my hand and closed my fist around it," I say in amazement, exploring the street for any signs of life that's not V or me. "I opened my hand, and this dropped out."

Veronica looks at the paper, dumbfounded.

"Well." She quickly recovers. "You going to look at it or what?"

I take a deep breath and pick up the paper in my flesh-and-blood right hand and begin unfolding. It's all scrunched and knotted, like someone had fun when they balled this up.

I smooth it out on my knee and make out the hand-writing:

You can save him.
He is still within reach.
He will not be for long.
Once he is gone,
he is gone forever.

Meet me at Mandrake Meadow.
You can save him.

"You can save him," Veronica reads out loud from over my shoulder. "Whoa. That's spooky."

I stare at the words, reading them over and over:

You can save him.

Save him.

You can save him.

I can save him.

"Where's this Mandrake Meadow?" I ask.

"So you're not at all sketched out by this, um, how do I say, hands-free messaging?"

I shrug. "Got my attention, didn't it? I mean, yeah, it's spooky. But I've gotta see what this is about, don't you think?"

"But why is this note anonymous? There's just a lot of red flags. If they were trying to help, why not just come, like, in the light of day? And, like, visible?"

"There's lots of questions I need to ask, I guess. But V, I just can't help but think I *should* be able to reach him somehow. Your pops told me my hand is half trapped in the Realm. If *my hand* is in the Realm, and we know *Pops* is in the Realm, well . . ."

. . . I can save him . . .

"I hear you," says V. "Mandrake Meadow . . . That, I don't know. But it sounds kind of familiar? Like something I just heard, or saw . . . God, it's at the tip of my tongue . . ." And then something dawns on her. "King, you still have that map?"

The map. "V, I can't believe I forgot all about it! I even forgot to mention it to your dad," I say, and dig in my back pocket for the old folded-up piece of paper. I'm shaking my head at myself. "Jeez, I even tried to recount everything that happened for him, *twice*."

"Sure," V says dubiously. "You forgot all about it."

"No, really—"

"I get it, King. You wanted to keep something to yourself. I'd probably do the same thing."

Did I keep the map to myself on purpose? I wonder.

She gets her fingers on the map and tracks quickly to *Mandrake Meadow*, listed just a few blocks away from *Pocket Playground* with a little illustration of wavy lines that must represent grass or something.

"There," she says. "Strange. I don't know when this map was made, but there's no meadow there now."

I scan the names on the map. Some look familiar, but most of them don't.

"Wow," I say. "So whoever slipped me that note must know about this map, and know that we have it."

It gets so quiet between us for a moment that I swear I hear crickets, even though there's no crickets in Brooklyn.

"It just gets creepier, huh, King?" V finally speaks. "I'd tread very carefully if I were you. And don't stay out here all night. If anybody needs a decent night's sleep, it's you."

V goes to her room to either fall asleep or watch anime on her laptop. Whichever comes first, she says.

I spend another couple minutes out on the stoop before I tiptoe upstairs, doing my best not to wake Ma. I take each step in super-slow-mo, being extra quiet but also making sure I don't stub my toe or trip on anything. The steps are so noisy, it doesn't seem to matter. I hold on to the banister, but it's loose and that makes the whole staircase creak and moan, so I rush up to the second floor like the ship's about to go down.

I hear another noise, like pipes squeaking in the distance. At first, I think it's this cranky old brownstone acting up again, but as I get closer to my mom's room, it's not that. It's her. She has a light on. She's awake.

Her door is open a crack. I ease closer.

And I realize she's crying.

I can just make her out, lying under the covers.

She's all the way on her side of the king-size bed. The entire other side of the bed is untouched. Like even now, after all these years, she sleeps as if he's still there. Like he could walk through this door this instant and climb into bed with her and she wouldn't even have to move an inch.

She's crying because she misses him. And being here makes it worse.

I realize I'm not breathing. Hearing her cry just stole the breath right out my chest.

I slip into my room and close the door as gently as possible and I get in my bed and I cry, too.

Because after all this, all I went through with the Mercury and the box and the hand and learning about the Realm . . .

He's still gone.

After Ma spent years working to put food on the table and then got the strength to face Echo City and everything she's lost and come back home for her dream to run a café . . .

He's still gone.

After learning that V's mom abandoned her and that

as bad as I think I have it sometimes, others have it worse, and at least my pops was around to raise me and he was a good man and he loved me . . .

He's still gone.

At that point, nothing else matters.

He's still gone, and I have to bring him back.

And not just for me.

THE REST OF Saturday night to Sunday morning is spent trying to wrestle my squirming body and hyperactive mind into something resembling rest.

When the blinds glow with the rising sun, it's a relief that I can stop pretending to sleep.

And start thinking of a way to get out of the house.

By the time Mom comes to get me for this chore or another, she sees me wearing high-tops, ball shorts, a tank top, and exactly one white glove.

"Morning, Ma, is it cool if I go hit the playground with Too T—Eddie today?"

She's taken aback to see me so ready to go.

"W-well, sure, honey." The ends of her lips curl up in a smile.

Then I remember her last night, crying quietly on her side of the bed while that massive empty space lay next to her.

"You two made plans?" she asks.

"Yeah." The lie comes quickly. "He's coming by, I should just call him, tell him I'm ready."

"My boy, you sure are in a rush. Don't you want breakfast?"

"Breakfast—of course. Sure."

"You two are picking up right where you left off, huh?"

"Yeah, Ma. I mean, it's good to be back, you know? This place—it's weird and all, but it feels like home. You think?"

Her mouth drops open. She's probably not sure how to respond.

"I think we'll be okay," I say with a shrug. "That's all."

"Good, King . . . I'm glad." She looks like she doesn't know what's gotten into me, but she'll take it.

BREAKFAST FEELS LIKE it takes forever. Too Tall doesn't show up until close to noon. Leaves Mom plenty of time to come up with chores for me to do. By the time Too Tall gets to our door, even he's surprised by how ready I am to go.

"Okay, bye, Ma, bye, Uncle!" I say, and I'm halfway out the door before they can say anything back.

"Whoa, can I, like, say hi to your peeps, man?" says Too Tall.

"Later."

"King!" my mom calls from the top of the stairs.

I freeze in mid-dash. "Yeah, Ma?"

She hesitates like she's not sure what to say. "Be safe."

Strange how her words and that somber look land like a jackknife to the gut, but I still manage to say, "Of course," with an eye roll like I'm just *so* over it.

"And be back by five for dinner. No later."

"Hi, Miss James!" Too Tall shouts with a wave like he's signaling an airplane.

"Hi, Eddie!"

"Let's go," I hiss at him, and flee down the block.

"What's the rush, King?" asks Tall, catching up. "Pickup games won't run for real for another few hours."

I want to tell him about everything. So much has

happened even in the handful of hours since I've seen him. But all that comes out my mouth is "Stuff. A lotta big-time stuff, man, I need to update you. Let's get off of Ricks before Ma thinks of some reason I need to come back."

It's just days before the Fourth of July and I feel like I could melt into the sidewalk. The concrete and brick and asphalt all bake in the sun and you can see the heat moving through the air like opening an oven door. Heat like you're wearing another person on you at all times. I'm already sweating as we round the corner to Thurston Avenue.

The names of all the streets of Echo City are vivid in my mind after studying that map.

"Okay, tell me, tell me!" says Tall.

"On the way."

"Where to? I know Echo City like the back of my hand."

"To Mandrake Meadow."

"Huh? Where's that?"

"Thought you knew Echo City like the back of your hand," I say with a grin.

Too Tall examines the back of his hand like he just noticed it for the first time. "To be honest with you? I, like, never look at the back of my hand."

"You know what I mean."

"No, really—look at those little hairs on my knuckles. You got those?"

"Wouldn't know."

I take the map out of my pocket—those deep pockets they put in basketball shorts—and open the map in front of him.

"Okay, King-crazy, what am I supposed to be looking at?"

I tap a finger to *Mandrake Meadow*.

Too Tall scrunches up his face like he's reading the last line in an eye exam. "Okay . . . Yeah, I know where that is. But it's just, like, some old lot. Calling that a meadow— that's a stretch. You should see—it's like they demoed a building and just left the rubble laying there. Got all kinds of randos squatting, sketchy."

"Huh," I say, and reexamine the map.

"King, listen. I need you to back it up, I mean *all the way* up to the beginning."

"Okay, okay. Ready for it? I know where my pops is. My uncle told me."

"Yeah?" says Tall, keeping pace with me once again. "Wait, *what*?" he shouts when it dawns on him what I just said. "Your *pops*? That's huge, King, what'd he say?"

"He said, *Your father ain't exactly gone. But he ain't never coming back.*"

"Okay. Is that, like, some kinda riddle?"

"Well, it's hard to explain. You gotta promise this stays between us, okay?"

"Of course, my man. I already didn't tell *any* of my cousins about the fact that . . ." Tall eyes the strangers passing us on the street with suspicion. Then he mouths, *That-you-don't-have-a-hand.*

"Thanks, man. Let's walk and talk."

As I tell Tall all about the Realm, I check the map against the neighborhood, down Thurston Avenue, the main stretch of Echo City. Mandrake Meadow isn't the only thing on the map that isn't there now. All these spots on the map are different. What's called the *Red Room* on a map label is actually a dive bar. *The Double Rainbow* cashes checks. *The Flourish* is a bodega with a handful of people trying their luck on lotto tickets. *The Dead End*— an enclosed triangle with haunted houses like the Ghost Gaze, Lemur Leftovers, and the Jamaican spot, Duppy Conqueror—those ghost spots are just ghost, boarded up and abandoned. The *Devant Dollar Store* is a Family Dollar now. The *Davenport Brothers Furniture* store is a Raymour & Flanigan. *The Sawed Lady* is Bella's Beauty, and *Conjuror's Cuts* is a Supercuts. The *Eye of Agamoto* is called Sumi Sushi, *Fu Manchu Chow* is Han Dynasty, and *Marabout Middle Eastern Grill* is called Shawarma House.

Too Tall is sufficiently blown away by my explanation about the Realm, and my ability to both tell a story and check the map against the city at the same time.

"So your hand is part . . . in this *Realmy, realm-agic-y* place?"

"Yup."

"And that's where your pops went."

"That's what my uncle says."

"So in theory, you could, like, shake his hand or something?"

"See, that's what I'm thinking! Only I don't think my uncle wants me to try or anything."

"What makes you say that?"

"Well, he said, like, don't do that. Or anything with the hand or the Realm at all. He said he'd smell it. He's working on fixing it so I get my normal hand back."

"Boring."

"Agree. I mean, what's the harm in a little magic, right? I used it without realizing on Mint back at the Mercury—"

"Outstanding—much respect—"

"Thank you—and nothing bad happened then. I mean, I get that opening a *big* rift between our world and the Realm would be horrendous, but I asked my uncle about using *little* bits of magic here and there, and he got all funny about it. Like he thinks I'll try it."

"Well . . ."

"Well, yeah, I might. But just to get my pops back. I mean, can you imagine that? If I could bring him back—for mom and my uncles and *us*."

"Well, sure," Tall says, and thinks this over. "But you have no idea how to actually do that."

"Ah, here's the last part of my night. The Mandrake Meadow part."

"Good. I almost forgot."

"I'm sitting there on the stoop—it's like four in the morning. And I feel someone put a balled-up piece of paper in my hand—my Realm hand—but there's no one there! I can't see a thing, until I open my hand and this falls out."

I reach in my other pocket and show Tall the hand-written note.

"You can save him," Tall reads. "You *can save him*?"

"Right? I can save him!"

But Tall doesn't share my excitement. "Listen, King, this one feels a little sketchy to me."

"What do you mean?"

"First of all, this Mandrake Meadow is a sketch spot. But even this note? I don't know, man. Like, if it was on the up-and-up, why not just come to you, straight-up? Why all the hocus-pocus? Why didn't somebody sign the note?"

"Yeah, that's what Veronica said. I'm thinking, only one way to find out."

"King, I know you been out of Brooklyn for a few years now, but you got to be more suspicious about, well, most things. Especially strange things, like this. It could be a—"

"Don't say it could be a trap."

"It *could* be a trap. And we already *know* Mint and them are gunning for you. Mint seems like a tricky type, maybe he slipped you that note?"

"Tall, whoever gave me that note slipped it in my *Realm* hand. That means they got some kinda Realm power, or access at least. You really think Mint got it like that?"

"Look, this is all over my head. I'm just saying, it's over yours, too. You got to be careful."

Everyone's caution is frustrating me. *Does no one understand how important this is?*

"But what if what the note says is true? What if I can save him? And what about the part in the middle? *He is still within reach*," I recite. "*He will not be for long. Once he is gone, he is gone forever.* Tall, my uncle explained some things, but there's so much I don't understand about where my father is and what he's doing. If there's a chance, even a small chance, that note is true, then I need to find out."

He nods like he hears what I'm saying and takes a deep breath.

"We'll find out soon enough. We're here."

MANDRAKE MEADOW IS just as Too Tall described, though if a building were demoed here, I've never seen one so thoroughly pulverized before. The whole field is just *dust*. I can't even make out the shape of a brick or anything. It's just fine, dark gray grains that slope in mounds like a beach in the dead of night.

"I knew you couldn't keep away," says a familiar voice from behind us.

Veronica walks up in a baggy pair of ripped-up jeans and her hands in her pockets. She squints at me and shakes her head. "Let me ask you this. What would you do if I *didn't* cancel my plans to clean out the old chess masters at Pocket Playground, just to come watch your back? Don't answer that," she says before I could anyway. "I know. That's why I came."

"Thanks, V. I'm not gonna lie, I'm glad you're here," I say.

"Can I maybe try one more time to talk you out of, well, whatever terrible idea you're up to?"

I think about how to explain how important this is to me, without sounding childish.

Veronica sighs. "Save it. I get it. At least you brought along some muscle." She looks Too Tall up and down. "Mr., um, Appropriately Tall, was it?"

"Uh, it's Too Tall, actually," he mumbles.

"Okay, King," she says, and looks at the barren field. "We going to check this 'meadow' out or what?"

"Not much to check out," says Tall, his head swiveling, on the lookout.

We all scan the dusty lot.

"You guys don't remember anything else ever being here? Like a building?" I ask.

Too Tall and Veronica shrug.

"There had to be something. I mean, look, there's a bit of a wall over there—right?"

A short section of wall—or something like it—stands over on the other side of the field of dust.

"I guess . . . ," Tall says as he squints.

"Welp, only one way to know for sure," I say, and set out across the field.

V shrugs, following me. "Okay. Let's do it." Too Tall hesitates.

"It's okay, Tall," I call. "We'll check it out and be right back."

"Man . . . You lucky I'm rocking my beater shoes," he complains, but follows behind. "You don't know Mint and them like I do. Those dudes took a bad turn. Got, like, nothing to live for. I don't trust them. Just wish you wouldn't take these chances."

"You sound like my ma," I say.

"She sounds like a smart lady," says Veronica.

The wall stands like a ruin against the sky. The gray dust gets all in our shoe soles, laces, and even leaves a layer of film on my ankles. It smells like the stale debris around a construction site. As we get closer, I can make out a mural painted on what's left of the wall.

It's a painting of a meadow so vivid it could be a photograph. Green slopes, tall grass, reeds and dandelions restless in the wind. There are patches of flowers that look like angry black roses. V says those look like mandrakes maybe. The whole meadow feels like it's moving, only you just missed it. Like you can feel the twitch of a blade of grass in the corner of your eye. There's charcoal clouds that shift like a coming storm.

I stare and stare. Feels like I could stare forever. Like the green slopes keep unfolding deeper and deeper.

"*Wow*," says Too Tall. "Whoever's painting these is, like, *good*."

"Like the one back at the Mercury," I say.

"Yeah. The one I was staring at when I fell on you . . ."

"Of my father and Maestro. But look at that . . ."

There's an object on one of the sloping green patches of grass. It's a hat. I get all the way up to it and look carefully. A porkpie hat. With a card in the band.

It's . . . "That's my dad's hat!"

"Wow," says Veronica.

"What's that, now?" says Tall.

"Right there—look!" I say.

"How do you know that's your dad's?" asks Tall.

"Because look at the card there, tucked in the band. You see the insignia, with the bear's head? That's the Joker from Hooker's Vanishing Deck! It's one of my dad's old tricks."

"Well, how do you suppose your pop's hat got in this here meadow?"

Something to be said for Too Tall—instead of trying to tell me that it's not real, it's just a painting, he wants to know how the hat got there.

"I mean, Dad was wearing that hat when he jumped through the Mirror."

"Whoa," says Tall.

Could that hat be in the Realm? Does that mean this meadow is showing us the Realm somehow?

What if . . .

As crazy as the idea seems, I pull the glove off my ghost hand.

"King—didn't my dad say not to use that hand?" shoots Veronica. "At least, that's what he told me."

Too Tall realizes what I'm doing and covers his mouth.

I reach with my phantom fingers to the mural, right on the image of the hat . . .

And my hand hits a solid wall.

"Okay. Maybe I got carried away," I admit.

Too Tall shrugs. "Worth a shot, I guess."

"Right idea," says a voice from nowhere. "Wrong equipment."

Too Tall told me so.

Mint steps out from behind the wall.

MINT IS PALE and washed-out like he's made of gray construction paper, though his green eyes are even brighter in the sun.

"I told you, King," says Tall. "It's a goose chase. We outta here."

Mint raises his hands like he means no harm. "No goose. No chase. No clown. No jokes." His voice is steady, like how he spoke to his crew back at the Mercury, *Smoke them out.* Like it was nothing. Like talking to us now is nothing.

"What do you want, Mint?" asks Veronica in a bored tone.

Mint fixes his eyes on me. "My boss wants you," he says.

"Who's your boss?"

"You'll find out when you come with me."

Veronica and Too Tall fold their arms like a pair of bodyguards.

"That don't cut it, chief," says Too Tall.

"Do better," says Veronica.

"Can he speak for himself?" asks Mint.

"He can. But we're, like, his lawyers on this side of King's County," says Tall.

"Why doesn't your boss come here himself?" I say. "And why do you have a boss anyway? Is bugging me, like, your job somehow?"

Mint holds out his hands. "I got no answers for you. I'm just an escort today."

"Mint, I know we barely know each other," says Veronica. "Just around the neighborhood here and there. But take it from me. You look terrible."

Mint blinks like a lizard and looks at me.

Tall says to me under his breath, "He's bad news, King. Bet you anything he wants to take you to that creepy spot on Torrini Boulevard. My cousin warned me not to go near that house. Says kids go in and don't ever come back out."

"What does your boss want?" I ask.

"Says the note should speak for itself," answers Mint.

"Well, if the boss is not here, why'd the note say to come here?"

"Isn't it obvious?" he asks, and then turns to admire the mural, with the porkpie hat on the sloping grass. "Boss thought you'd recognize this."

I keep my poker face as flat as his tone. *Reveal nothing.*

"*You* painted this?" asks Too Tall.

"Me? Do I look like that freak?" Mint chuckles without smiling. His laughter sounds strange, like trying to start a car when the engine won't turn over. "May not be CCTV, but it's as close as we get."

Too Tall is puzzled. "CC . . . TV?" he repeats, squinting at the mural.

"If you Einsteins need it spelled out for you, take a class. I'm here for Kingston. You coming or not?"

Veronica holds up a finger in front of Mint's face like an exclamation point. "'Scuse us. We need a word with our client. King, sidebar."

She hooks one of my arms and one of Tall's and takes

us out of Mint's earshot. She whispers, "Okay. You're not seriously considering going with him, are you?"

One look at me and she knows the answer.

"King!" says Tall. "For one, you're crazy."

"I know this is all a bit creepy," I say.

"There has got to be a creepier word than *creepy* to describe how creepy this all is," says Veronica.

"What's for two?" I ask Tall.

"Huh?"

"You said, 'King, for one, you're crazy.' So what's 'for two'?" I say.

"For two, this is *all* crazy!" says Tall. "I mean, that dude's neck scar over there? Looks like somebody went and killed that dude but he forgot to die! That could be this 'boss,' for all we know."

"Right—for all we know. But we don't know. I came this far, Tall, I need to find out. Listen, if I don't come back—"

"What?" says Veronica.

"I'm saying, if I don't come back—"

"Oh no. That's not how this works," she says, and doubles back to Mint. "Okay, green eyes. King is coming. But so are we. So you and your boss got to deal. Deal?"

"I'll have to ask," says Mint.

"Fine, ask your supervisor for permission. But if you want King, you get us, too."

AN OLD THREE-STORY building stands out on Torrini Boulevard, separated by narrow alleyways on either side from the other buildings. Usually in Echo City, the buildings line up right next to one another, but not this one. There's a yard out front with yellow grass, dirt patches, and crunchy leaves that've laid here dead since last fall. There's an overgrown driveway and a car that probably hasn't been used in decades, but it looks like it's been centuries. The metal wheels bite the dirt and the tires droop in the dead grass like puddles.

I hear Too Tall's lungs heaving by my ear. I look up at the house and I almost lose my nerve. We approach the front door. It's huge and towers over even Too Tall. There's a crystal mounted atop the entrance. I point to the crystal and look at Tall. He nods. It's just like the crystal he had back at the theater. I wonder if he's still got it, but I don't want to ask in front of Mint.

There are white columns on either side like a pair of

fangs. The white paint is chipped and the panels are decaying. Ivy covers the building like some tentacled monster. Mint pounds a fist on the door and slips inside. We shoot nervous glances at one another.

"Thank you guys," I whisper, and part of me wishes they weren't here. I'm glad they are, but if anything bad happens to them? I'd never forgive myself.

The door opens up like a slow yawn and Mint's voice tells us to "Come in."

We take uneasy steps through the gloomy archway. It smells like wet, rotten wood mixed with old washed-up-actress perfume.

Urma Tan is at the top of the stairway in front of us. Maestro's assistant. The one who went through the Mirror that night at the Mercury.

Last time I saw her was the last time I saw my dad.

MY MOUTH DROPS open. I can't believe my eyes.

She should not be here. She should be in the Realm, with Maestro and my father.

But she *is* here. It's her, there's no mistaking. She looks older, of course, but it's her. Same pale eyes and pale skin. Her hair is all the way white now. She takes a step down the stairs in a nightgown and it looks like she's floating.

"*The She-Wizard . . . ,*" Too Tall whispers.

"Is that . . . ," asks Veronica, her question trailing off.

"Welcome," Urma says, and extends a hand, her long, pale fingernails like a drawn blade.

"You—you're Urma Tan," I manage to say.

I give her hand an awkward half squeeze.

"I am."

"But . . . you're not supposed to be here. You're supposed to be gone, with my dad," I say.

"Hello, Kingston. Veronica." She takes the hand of my cousin, who also looks dumbfounded. "And who is this?"

Too Tall introduces himself.

"Thank you all for coming. I'm sure you have questions, and I'm happy to explain. Come," she says. "Have a seat."

Mint leaves us as Urma leads the way into a sitting room that feels like no one has sat in for years. There's a thick shag carpet and a couple of couches, and all of it is beige. The couch cushions look comfortable but have these springs that stick you where you sit.

"Some tea?" she offers. There's a little teapot on a silver tray on the coffee table. I feel like I'm at my grandma's. Too Tall looks at it like it's a tray full of rat poison.

"No thanks. Um, where's my dad?" I ask.

She purses her thin lips. "I don't know," she says with regret in her voice.

"But you both went through that Mirror," I say.

"Kingston, I think you ought to listen to what I have to say. Then maybe you'll understand where I've been and what I'm doing here. Tell me, first, what do you know about the Realm?"

Too Tall gives me a wary look that says, *Don't give anything away.*

I almost say *I know my dad is there*—thinking, I don't know much else, I don't know what he's doing there, or what actually *is* there—but Veronica cuts me off.

"Wait, King." She turns to Urma Tan. "Lady, with all due respect, you asked him here. You're the one that *went* to the Realm. You slipped him that note somehow, into his Realm hand. Neat trick and all, but you're the one that should be telling us about the Realm."

"Fair point," says Urma, clicking her teeth. "It's hard to know where to begin."

"Maybe start with how you got back to our reality?" I say.

"One can get from the Realm and back with a portal, like Maestro's Mirror. Creating a portal is difficult, but not impossible."

"And I can do it? I can bring my dad back?" I ask, trying to keep the excitement out of my voice.

"Yes," she says. "And I can help you."

"How?" asks Veronica. "And why? I mean, what's in it for you?"

"I can help you make the portal. That requires some doing. And as for what's in it for me, well, that's a longer story. In order to understand why I need your help, you must understand the nature of the Realm."

"Okay, so what is it?" I ask.

"And don't just say it will wreck reality as we know it if we open a portal," says Veronica. "We get it."

"I would never tell you that," says Urma. "In order to understand the Realm, first you must understand the nature of magic. You see, real magic can do anything you could possibly dream. Only, magic doesn't dream. It doesn't imagine, or think, or anything we people do. It can't. Magic is not people. However, it *likes* people. Without people, who would care about magic? Without people, who would dream up the impossible? Without people, magic doesn't really know what to do. So you could say magic is dependent on people. And in that way, the Realm is very suggestible." Urma turns her pale eyes to me. I feel like I'm under a hot lamp. "When one opens a rift between worlds, the Realm absorbs all it sees. And copies it. Creates an echo. A moment in time that lives forever. Does that make sense?"

Veronica and Tall look about as lost as I feel.

"Um, sort of," I say. "So it's, like, a copy of our world? With, like, places and people and things?"

"And Not Not Ray's?" asks Too Tall. "I mean, Poppa James gotta be eating something."

I have to admit, it's nice to think my father might be in a place that resembles our reality. I realize that I've been imagining him sort of floating in a netherworld, with solar systems and shooting stars and empty space like he's alone in the universe.

"When a rift opens, the Realm copies. So if there's a rift near the pizza place, then yes. There's pizza."

"And you were *there*?" says Veronica.

"How did you get back?" I ask.

Urma stands. She opens her robe and reveals a crystal dangling around her neck by a thin chain. The crystal is big like costume jewelry with a blue light glowing in its center like a cold star.

Too Tall slaps a hand over his mouth. It looks just like the crystal he found under the stage.

"This may be hard to believe, but here's the truth. I know the Realm because the Realm made me," says Urma Tan. "I'm not the Urma you think I am. I'm not from this world."

"Huh?" comes out my mouth.

"Um, excuse me?" says V.

My uncle's words come back to me. *Say there was a fish, ended up on our side of the glass . . .*

"The night of the fire at the Mercury, the Urma of your world went through the Mirror and to the Realm with Maestro and your father." She shrugs and paces like a cat. "That wasn't me. I'm a different Urma Tan."

"**Wait, what?**" I sputter.

Veronica folds her arms. "Does that *not-of-this-world* bit work on Mint and those followers of yours?"

"I'm too old to play games with children," Urma says. "I'm too weak, and I don't have the time. Remember you asked if the Realm had people in it? Well, it does. I was one of them. I'm not the your-world Urma Tan. That Urma is there, somewhere, best of luck to her. I'm a copy." She flashes jazz hands. "*Ta-da.*"

"You're saying that wasn't even you onstage four years ago?" I ask.

"Correct. We just did the teleportation trick, and I was hiding."

The three of us are stunned silent. I don't even know where to begin with this one.

"Maestro led me to this reality to use me in his magic act," she says like that should explain everything. Then she sees how unconvinced we are. "I know. It's a lot. I have something to show you. It might help you understand."

Urma opens a pair of cabinet doors. There's an old television set there, and a stack of homemade DVDs. She puts one in the DVD player and pokes a couple buttons on the remote.

There's a stage. It looks like the Mercury before the fire. But I can tell it's not that night. The lighting is different, like it's a matinee. Maestro waltzes out to rounds of applause in his spooky, mirrored magic-man mask. Urma is behind him. She's wearing black elbow-length gloves, a white halter top, and a bow tie.

"I look good, don't I?" says Urma in the living room, watching the screen. "Well, *she* looks good, anyways. We were identical."

She hits the fast-forward button. Maestro's act flies by on the screen. He buzzes around the stage doing illusions with metal rings, works the crowd, gets back onstage, does card tricks with a volunteer from the audience, shows him a card, pretty standard stuff.

Urma clicks a button and the DVD plays at regular speed for this next part. I recognize the setup right away; they did this trick the night of the fire.

Urma, on the stage, wheels out a tall cabinet with two doors that stands a head taller than Maestro. There's no chatter, just instrumental music that buzzes heavy with bass. Urma moves half like a dancer and half like she's showing cars at a car show. She wheels another cabinet out that's identical to the first one. Then a third cabinet that she sets between the other two. Maestro gestures for the audience to watch carefully as he enters the first cabinet on the left. Urma joins him. She pulls a rope from inside somewhere and ties Maestro's wrists up. Maestro pretends to struggle. Urma closes the cabinet doors on him. Then she steps inside the cabinet in the center and waves her arms around "magically," and the cabinets to either side of her rise off the ground (on wires; I can see the wires). She picks a white sheet up off the floor and holds it high so you can't see her. She shakes the sheet once, twice. And reveals . . . Maestro. He's standing there now, twirling the sheet, and posing in the center cabinet to applause. Urma is gone. He points to the first cabinet, where he was just tied up. The doors fly open and it's empty. He points to the third cabinet, to his left. The doors fly open and there's Urma. Posing. Cheesing.

"*Voilà*," Urma says, pausing the DVD as her old self takes a bow. "Teleportation. Maestro's best trick. None of the old magicians could figure out how he did it."

"Wait, so you're saying that's *you*? And there's *another* Urma on the stage somewhere?" I ask.

"We would switch roles. Sometimes I would be the one hiding behind the cabinet. Sometimes I'd be the girl getting the applause."

"But you could be look-alikes," Veronica says. "You could even be her twin for all we know. I'm saying, how does this all mean you're from *the Realm*?"

"My dear, I didn't believe it myself. When I first met the other Urma, *I* even thought I was the original Urma, and she the copy. But Maestro showed me it's true."

"Wait, so you're saying there's copies of *everything* in our world?" asks Too Tall. "Like, there's a Realm Kingston, there's a Realm me?"

"Certainly."

Too Tall is trying to process all this. "So it's a multiverse sort of situation?"

"Come on," says V. "You're not buying this, are you?"

"I have no reason to lie to you, Veronica," says Urma.

"I bet you do," V shoots back. "I bet you have some reason you lured my cousin to this house."

"You're right, Veronica. There is a reason I brought you here. And a reason I'm telling you everything I know." Urma holds the crystal around her neck in her hands. "Because I can't live without *this*."

"I found one of those under the stage," says Tall. "What is it?"

"This crystal, like me, is *of the Realm*. It enables me to live in your reality. Without it, I would wither up and expire. It's like pure Realm energy, concentrated. It's made of the stuff of my world, and it keeps me going."

"Okay," I say. "But what's that got to do with me?"

"When Maestro first brought me to this world, he had this box. It was a small box, made of wood, but enchanted in such a way that it could reach the Realm without opening a rift. Maestro would put a crystal inside and it would come out full of Realm energy. It's a small thing, but it means everything to me."

"And this box . . . ," I say.

She looks back at the television like she's remembering something. "It turned out it was Preston's box, and he took it back. The box you found at the Mercury, Kingston."

"Okay," says Veronica, losing her patience. "So you want the box King found. Is that it? Well, you can't have it. Because we don't even have it. Can we go now?"

"You don't have it?" Urma asks with a nervous chuckle. She digs her nails against the crystal around her neck. "But I'm sure you can get it, no?"

"Wait, I don't understand," I say. "If you need these crystals to survive, what have you been doing since my dad disappeared? I mean, you haven't had the box this whole time."

"It hasn't been easy. When Maestro opened the portal the night of the fire, that rift created heaps of crystal. I gathered them. I've kept them. There's crystals all around us, in this house. I'm surviving, but barely. I haven't left the house since that day four years ago, Kingston. I need that box to live. If you would bring it to me, I will show you how to retrieve your father from the Realm."

It sounds good. Too good. I want to believe she can help me. I want to believe that giving her the box would solve everything. But I have this nagging feeling. I remember my uncle's warning. *That fish out of water I was talking about? Imagine it's more like a shark. And you're just chum.*

"My uncle has the box, Miss Tan. If you can help us get my dad back, I'm sure he'll let you hold the box," I say, though I'm not exactly sure of anything my uncle will or won't do. "I can ask him," I offer.

This doesn't seem to satisfy Urma.

"But how can you be sure he'll be reasonable? Maybe," she says like the idea just occurred to her, "you can sneak it for me?"

"Are you asking me to swipe it from my uncle, to give to you?"

"We're not stealing from my father for you, lady," says Veronica.

"Of course. Of course, I understand," Urma says. "Could you do me one favor, then?"

She removes the crystal from around her neck by its chain and dangles it in front of us.

My eyes are drawn to the light in the center that looks like a tiny star.

"Look at the light."

The crystal swings.

Back . . .

And forth . . .

"Look at the light," she repeats.

And I'm so, so sleepy.

Eyelids so heavy they fall shut.

21

WAIT FOR YOUR father . . .

Wait for your father . . .

Wait for your father to go to sleep. Search his workshop for the Magician's Lost and Found. Bring the box and the Watch of 13 to me. Wait for your father to go to sleep. Search his workshop for the Magician's Lost and Found. Bring the box and the Watch of 13 to me. Wait for your father to go to sleep . . .

My eyes open. I have to resist the urge to sleep. It's hard. I want to sleep very badly. But I can't. I know I can't. This isn't right at all.

I'm on the beige couch next to Veronica and Too Tall. Too Tall is fast asleep against the armchair next to the couch. We're surrounded by Mint and the boys from the theater. Urma Tan is in front of them, standing over us. She's dangling the crystal in front of Veronica. It's rocking back and forth, back and forth. My cousin is in some kind of trance. Urma is speaking to her.

" . . . bring the box and the Watch of 13 to me."

"He's awake!" Mint shouts.

It takes me a second to realize he's talking about me.

"What?" says Urma.

"Kingston—he's awake!" Mint repeats, pointing at me. I've never heard him sound so surprised.

Urma's pale eyes turn to me. "How in the world?" she says, almost to herself.

"His hand's glowing," growls Mint.

"Indeed," says Urma.

"You said he's not strong enough to resist yet—" says Mint.

Strong enough . . . yet? I look down, a step behind their conversation. My hand *is* glowing.

I get a jolt of awareness as everything that's going on around me clicks. Too Tall is asleep, Veronica is in a trance, I'm groggy, just waking up . . .

The crystal catches my eye. The chain sways and the light from inside the shard winks at me. It's like a star trapped in ice. I realize my hand is reaching for the light. My fingers are glowing blue beneath the glove. I feel like I'm in some sort of trance, but not the trance Urma was trying to put me in. The opposite of that. I can sense what she wants from me, but all this energy coming from my hand is resisting her. Power is gathering to my fingertips. I can detect the faintest shifts of breath on the air. It's like I can touch anything I want in the room without moving. Like I can touch the crystal . . .

It *leaps* from Urma's grasp and whips across the coffee table. I catch it as though I called it *straight to my hand*.

I stare at diamond-shaped crystal. I thought it would be cold, but it's warm to the touch.

I look up. Urma and the crew are as stunned as I am.

As I hold the crystal in my hand, away from Urma, she gasps and changes color. Her flesh turns that construction-paper gray. It happens as quick as if a rain cloud blocked the sun. Suddenly, she looks like she's not made of flesh and blood. You can see the edges of her skull beneath her skin like she's peeling. The strength leaves her body, and Mint catches her before she falls.

"V, Tall!" I shout as loud as I can. "Wake up! Run!"

They both snap to, shaking off the trance, blinking really fast.

"Wha—?" says Tall.

"What's going on?" says V.

"Run!" I shout again. I'm on my feet now.

They don't need to be told twice.

We break for the door. The crew is too stunned and confused to do anything about it.

"Kingston." I hear Urma's weak voice.

I stop at the entrance.

V and Tall burn past me, out into the yard.

I know I probably shouldn't, but I look back.

Mint and one of his boys hold Urma up beneath her arms. She looks so weak, a strong breeze could crush her.

"Please. Help me," she says. "And I can help you save him."

I look down at the crystal in my hand.

My thoughts collide in my mind.

King, you can't trust her. She tried to hypnotize you.

But she needs it to live . . .

Can she really open a portal?

Like the one my dad sacrificed himself to close?

But can I really save him?

The thoughts come too fast and I'm stuck not knowing what to do.

"King!" Veronica shouts from outside. "Come on, let's go!"

I take one more look at Urma, and I can see that she's suffering. That part is real.

I drop the crystal at my feet by the door and I'm gone.

ONCE I CATCH up to Tall and my cousin, we all jog together like we're fleeing a crime scene. I can tell everyone is really shaken up, because no one wants to be the first to talk about what just happened. I don't know how we decided where to go, or whether we even decided at all, or if the smell of comfort food, of baking crust and cheese drew us to Not Not Ray's on its own.

We don't even say a word until we're all sitting down with hot pizza.

"I mean, what's she even doing with *children* there?" Veronica blurts as she takes a bite out of her sausage-and-peppers slice.

"I don't know. It was so strange," I say, relieved to be able to talk about it.

"Too strange for me," says Tall. "King, you want to tell

us what went down back there? I can't remember much. Only that it got very weird, very quickly."

"She held out that crystal," I say. "Next thing I knew, we were all asleep."

Then my hand was glowing. That's what woke me up.

It stopped glowing when we hit Thurston Avenue, about when we were out of range of Urma.

"What was she doing to us?" Veronica asks, and she sounds concerned.

"She was telling you, over and over, to steal the box from your dad and bring it to her," I say. "The box, and the Watch of 13."

"Are you serious?" Veronica scowls in outrage. "So that nutty lady put programs inside my mind? King, that is the worst thing I've ever heard."

"But maybe I stopped it? I mean, I think I stopped it," I say.

"How can you know?" she asks.

"Yeah, did they program me, too, King?" asks Tall.

"I honestly don't know. I was out cold. They seemed really surprised when I woke up, even," I say. "I think my Realm hand, like, snapped me out of it."

"Maybe she's hypnotizing those kids," says Tall. "I

mean, why would they hang around her like that? What's she doing for them?"

It hadn't occurred to me. But he's got a point.

"But why?" asks V. "What does she get out of it?"

"And if she's such a master hypnotist, then why try and talk to me at all? Why tell us all that about the Realm and being a copy? Why not just start with the hypnosis?"

"It's not that easy," says V. "Hypnotists—they have to make you drop your guard. You can't just walk into a room with a crystal on a chain."

"Did you guys see what happened when the crystal *flew* to me?" I ask. "I mean, can we talk about that for a sec?"

"Yeah, I wasn't sure if I dreamed that. It's very hazy," says Tall.

"What, like, it came to you?" asks V.

"Yeah, guys, this hand is, like, breaking all kinds of laws of physics. I guess you were in a trance at the time. The crystal popped right out of her hand and into mine. And did you see what happened next? She collapsed. She turned gray. Like, grayer than Mint, her whole body. I thought her face was going to fall off."

"Yeah," says V. "So what?"

"Maybe she was telling the truth?"

"The truth about what, now?" asks Tall.

"About needing the energy from the crystals to survive. About the Realm. About . . . creating a portal to bring Dad back," I say. "I think she was maybe telling the truth, is all."

"King, you sound kinda desperate," says V.

"What? I don't mean I'm going to give her the box. I just mean, maybe she's telling the truth. That we can make a portal."

"*We* can make a portal?"

"Well, whoever. I mean, doesn't it make sense? If Maestro could do it, why can't we? That's the part where I feel like she was telling the truth. And it's just the kind of thing your father wouldn't want to tell me, thinking I'll do something stupid."

"Well, in fairness to my dad, you *are* doing stupid things. Maestro was a master magician. He studied for a lifetime in order to be able to make that Mirror." Veronica releases a breath. "Should we tell my dad about all this?"

"I don't know, V."

"Not that I'm saying we should—but why not?" she asks.

"Because he won't let me do it. He probably thinks

something bad will happen if I try to get Pop back, just 'cause I'm a kid."

"So you want to do this on your own? Without Urma's help or my dad's help?"

"You think I should trust Urma Tan?"

"Well, it seems like you sorta kinda are, if you don't want to talk to my dad about it. You're taking her word at face value."

"Not at face value. Not exactly. I don't want to give her the box."

"But you think the rest of what she said was true? What if she made all that up just to get this box from you?"

"It's possible. Of course it's possible. I just wish we knew more."

"What about those murals?" says Tall. "I mean, whoever's painting those can, like, *see* the Realm somehow. We've got to find *them*. 'Cause, Urma? Urma Tan is lying," says Tall.

"Right," says Veronica.

"Well, like we said, since we don't know exactly *what* she's lying about, it's a good idea. I mean, even she says those murals show the Realm," I say.

"Is there proof, though?" asks Tall. "Is there any other

proof that these murals are of the Realm, other than Urma
'Suspect' Tan's word?"

I shrug. "My dad's hat?"

"You mentioned that before," says V. "Why do you
think it's in the Realm?"

"He wore that hat when he performed at the Mercury.
Remember? When he jumped through the Mirror."

"Okay," says Tall. "So, Operation Find Us a Muralist is
officially in effect."

"Great," I say.

"Matteo!" Too Tall calls.

"Yes, my friend?" Matteo is knuckles deep in a round
heap of dough.

"You know who's been doing those murals around
town?"

"Murals . . . Like the one of the graveyard over by the
Dead End?"

"Yeah," says Tall with a quick wink to us. "That's the
one." Though I'm pretty sure he's just playing along.

"That mural is incredible. My son almost turned and
walked into it! Spooky," he says.

"You know who does those?"

He shrugs. "No clue," he says, and goes back to his
dough.

"Okay," says Veronica. "So what's our first stop?"

"Let me ask you guys this. Is there an art supply store in Echo City?" I suggest. "I'm saying, whoever this muralist is, they go through a ton of paint. Something tells me it's local."

CLEOPATRA'S ART SUPPLIES is a makeshift storefront on the ground floor of a warehouse. A little bell chimes when we open the door, but for now, we're the only ones in the store. Too Tall, Veronica, and I walk the aisles, scanning the drafting pencils, different sizes and types of paper, and all the spray cans of paint. Everything feels half done. A stack of sketch pads separates two aisles. The back of the store is just a hanging tarp.

"Wow, they just leave the spray paint cans out like that?" observes Too Tall. "Maybe our muralist just swipes them."

Veronica asks, "What makes you say that?"

"Well, it's like King said. Those murals we saw? That's a lot of paint to go through. Paint costs money. Unless it don't, you feel me?"

The art store smells like plaster dust, warehouse debris, and pencil shavings.

"Look back here!" Too Tall holds one of the hanging tarps in the back aside. "You're going to want to see this, I think."

I duck through the opening. There's another tarped-off area, but this space has paintings hung up on the walls. They're all of street scenes from Echo City, with the same sort of strong outlines and colors as the murals. It's the old nightlife from years ago, people out and about in cuff links and jazzman hats and frilly dresses and pearls and silver heels in front of bright storefronts and neon signs splashing color into each frame. As I'm looking at each painting, the storefront signs begin to feel familiar . . . *The Red Room, The Double Rainbow, The Flourish, Lemur Leftovers, The Sawed Lady Salon* . . . I quickly pull the old map out of my shorts pocket and match the names.

I gaze at the paintings some more as it hits me that this is the Thurston Avenue from my map.

"Um, can I help you?" a voice intrudes.

We're all caught off guard. I turn to see a bald, serious-looking Black girl, maybe fourteen or fifteen, staring at us like she's caught us all shoplifting.

"We were just admiring your artwork," says Veronica, the first of us to recover.

"This isn't my work. And this area is private."

"Right. Er, sorry," says Veronica.

"The art supplies are all out front," says the girl.

I take one last look at the paintings as we file back out through the tarp.

Too Tall clears his throat and puts on a smile so big it's like an instant light show. "We were wondering if you knew the person doing these incredibly fly murals around the neighborhood," he says in a smooth delivery.

"Can't say I do," the girl says in a bored voice. "Can I help you find some supplies?"

"Do you know the murals we're talking about?" I ask. "They're kind of amazing."

"Lots of murals in Brooklyn," she says.

I smell something funny about her reaction. Like she isn't even asking which murals or where they are or anything. Like she just wants us to go away.

"Well, could you tell us who did those paintings of Thurston Avenue back there?" I ask, with a little more firmness in my voice.

She looks at me then, as if for the first time, and something about my face seems to startle her. She lets out a tiny gasp and her eyes twitch wide for a second.

She recovers fast, but her reaction was obvious.

"What? Did you paint those?" I ask.

"N-no," she says. "The owner paints those." Her mouth opens like she wants to ask me something, and then she changes her mind.

"Can we talk to him?" I ask.

"Or *her*?" Veronica says, darting a look at me before winking at the girl.

But she isn't feeling the love from V, either. "No. You can't."

"Listen. I know this may sound silly, but it's *really* important that we talk to whoever is doing these paintings," I say in my best pleading voice.

Veronica chimes in. "We have reason—I mean, *good* reason—to think that the person who does these paintings can help us figure out some really tough stuff that we can't figure out any other way."

She's listening. She's not bought in, but she's listening. And I like her face when she's listening to us.

"It's about my father," I say. "He's gone now. But I need to know if he's safe."

"Who's your father?" she asks.

"Preston James. I'm Kingston, this is my cousin Veronica. That there is Too Tall."

"Howdy," says Tall.

She nods to each of us. "I'm Sula. Preston was your father?"

"He *is* my father."

"Huh," Sula says, still with that good hard look at me. "And that's your face," she says, almost to herself.

I shrug. "Only face I got."

Sula sighs like she's about to do something she will regret. "I think you'd better follow me."

She turns on a dime and heads toward the back.

Veronica, Too Tall, and I all hesitate.

"You coming?" asks Sula.

She holds the tarp open, and waves.

We follow her down a hallway and up a temporary staircase to a platform. I notice her arms are muscular and she moves like an athlete. We turn another corner and enter a big room, lit by a lone bulb.

There's a wall with a just-finished mural.

Everyone is speechless.

There, painted on the wall, is *me*.

My face.

No question.

And I know exactly when it was.

Yesterday. I'm in the trapdoor chamber below the stage at the Mercury Theater. My hand is in the box. The Magician's Lost and Found, at least that's what Urma Tan called it, is painted huge. Like the box is falling toward the viewer. I'm behind the box with my hair crazy and my eyes bugging out. I'm stumbling over the box, my wrist disappeared inside.

Too Tall stares at the mural from inches away like he's just putting it together. "I was there," he whispers, and points to the corner where his sneaker just makes it into the frame.

There's a boy sitting at a table in front of the mural. He's covered in paint, and eating cereal. He's also bald, and his face is a dead ringer for Sula's.

"This is my brother, Sol," says Sula with a hand on his shoulder. "Sol, this is Kingston James. Preston's son." Her heavy-lidded eyes land on me. "Kingston, Maestro was our father."

IT TAKES A good minute for everything that's happening to sink in.

I'm looking from Sula to Sol, comparing them to my memories of Maestro's face.

Too Tall is still staring at the mural, paying special attention to the footwear in the background.

Sula is pacing and shaking her head. Worried about something.

Sol is staring at me even harder than I'm staring at him.

I realize it's weird to just look at another person's face for whole seconds on end, but in that moment, I don't care. Sol doesn't seem to care, either.

Maestro's children, I think. *Does the rivalry pass on from parent to child?*

And then I think, *But who could understand what I'm going through better than them?*

"Man, this mural is, like, good," says Too Tall. "I mean, really good. Kid even got the stitching right on my Concord 11s."

"How did you see this?" I ask Sol. "This just happened. Like, yesterday."

His eyes go wide. His dark pupils glimmer in the light like a pair of blackberries.

"How did you know I was there? When did you paint—" And I realize by his blank look that he's not going to answer, or say anything. "When did he paint this?" I turn to Sula.

"Yesterday. He was sleeping all day, which he does a lot, and then he woke up about six and he just started painting. Didn't stop for three hours," she says.

Veronica asks, "Your brother does all of these murals around the neighborhood?"

Sula glances at Veronica like she's trying to figure out friend from foe.

"I'm Veronica. Kingston's cousin. My father isn't

a magician like you guys, though. He's a trick builder. Which may be the only thing worse than a magician."

Sula breaks a grin. "Maybe. We'll have to compare notes sometime. But yes—my brother is Echo City's little phantom muralist. Where you may just see a wall, he sees a field of flowers."

I point to the mural. "I was there, yesterday, right when you said he woke up. That happened under the stage at the Mercury. Sula, everything in your brother's mural happened yesterday, to us."

Sula nods, taking it in.

"Well, to him everything he paints is really happening, whether it happens here or there," she says.

"You mean the Realm, don't you? You know about it?" I say.

"Do I know about the Realm?" Sula paces around the paint cans. "Does a butcher's kid know about a T-bone?" she asks me.

I shrug. "My dad never told me anything about it."

"Maybe. Or maybe you know more than you realize."

"I don't know. My dad was kinda big on protecting us."

"Can't say the same," says Sula. "But I didn't get the worst of it. My brother takes that honor."

I look into the kid's blackberry eyes, wondering what they've seen.

"I'm not sure if you already know this," Sula says carefully. "I feel I should tell you. You opened a rift to the Realm yesterday. Did you know that?"

"I . . . No," I say. "I did not know that."

Veronica shakes her head along with Too Tall.

"Oh," says Sula. "Yikes. That's all my brother paints. Scenes he sees in the Realm. So you didn't mean to do that?"

I look back up at the painting. "Does it look like I know what I'm doing?" I ask.

"To be honest with you, no. Guess I was hoping you did. It can be bad news, to mess with the Realm when you don't know what you're doing. Or even when you do know what you're doing, really. Nothing good ever happens."

"How does your brother see into the Realm?" asks Veronica.

"He just does. He's not what you'd call normal."

"This day is not what I'd call normal," Too Tall mutters.

"Listen, it's a long story. I've got some chocolate milkshakes in the fridge. I can shut down the store. You got time?"

We all nod. It's a better offer than we expected.

"So you *know* about the two Urmas? *Wow*," Sula says, taking a sip of chocolate milkshake. We all sit on empty plaster buckets on the warehouse floor. We've spent the last hour or so talking. Turns out Sol and Sula are both thirteen years old, Sol just looks younger. We told her about our trip to Urma's house on Torrini Boulevard. "That's going to make this story way easier to tell. Basically, we're both Maestro's kids," Sula says simply. "The real Urma Tan is my mother. The Realm Urma—the one you met earlier today, apparently—that's Sol's mother."

"Wait, what?" I say.

"That's a new one on me," says V.

Too Tall examines Sol's face.

"I don't know, bud. I think you look like your daddy," says Tall.

"So your mom *and* dad are in the Realm, just like my dad?" I say. "Realm Urma said that she can help us make a portal and bring them home."

There's a look of fear in Sula's eye as she shakes her head. "You *can't* trust her," she says.

"Right." Too Tall and V agree with Sula on that one.

"No, you don't understand. She isn't human." Sula turns to Veronica. "She only seems like a real person."

"You mean how she's some kinda Realm zombie?" asks Too Tall. "No offense," he says to Sol.

"Call her what you like. Trust me, he's not offended. I'm more of a mom to him than she ever was," says Sula. "She uses the power in those crystals to control and drain the children around her. It's how she stays looking like herself. Without feeding off their youth, she'd look as gray as those kids."

"I wondered what was happening to them," says Veronica, understanding.

"Mint and the rest of them all think they're learning some ancient magic, meanwhile she's just feeding off them. But she's running out of time, her Realm energy is depleted. It's been four years since anyone's opened the Realm, started a new echo. That is, until you showed up," she says, cutting her eyes at me.

"Why kids?" asks V.

"It's their youth, I think, that sustains her. Most of the kids come off the street around here, no family. She teaches them about crystals and shows off her 'powers.' Those crystals are the only thing keeping her alive. Somehow, they hold energy longer with the kids around. She has this *thirst*, like a vampire from another reality. She, like, drinks your life force. And you don't even know it's happening," says Sula.

"It happened to you?" asks V.

"And Sol. Look, I know you guys probably think you had a weird childhood, with magicians and trick builders and everything. But imagine there's two of your mom, and you have to pretend one doesn't exist."

"Okay," I say. "You win."

"We always wondered why Sol was sick a lot, and he had that gray look, you know, how the boys around her now look. That's how Sol used to look, too."

Sol flashes a healthy grin and pinches his own cheek, like, *Look how hearty I am these days.* He gets a smile out of me, V, and Tall.

"Just before the night of the Mercury, I told my father that Realm Urma was draining Sol," says Sula. "He didn't believe me, at first. But I think he was trying to return her to the Realm, before everything went wrong."

"Why do you say that?" I ask.

"Maestro—my father—I think made that portal that night to send Realm Urma back to the Realm, where she belongs. But somehow it was *my* mom that went through the Mirror. The rest is history. I think *she* pushed my mom through with her magic, somehow," says Sula. There's no doubt who *she* refers to.

"*She* hypnotized me to get me to steal from my father for her," says V. "Or, she tried to. Still not sure if it worked." She shrugs.

"I'm so sorry. She's hurt a lot of people, especially her own son. Sol was born with a gift and a curse. Sol gets these visions, and they're so intense they only go away if he paints them. It's like he needs to obsess over the image, and spend days with it, then it leaves him alone."

"You think it's because his mother is a Realm echo of the real Urma?"

"I think so," says Sula. "Kid's lucky to be here, whatever that means. It's like his body is here, but his mind is in the Realm. Like he's in two places at once."

Sol startles me for a second. He's pulled his headphones off and he's tugging at the white glove on my left hand.

I think I get it. He wants me to take the glove off.

He was listening the whole time. He knows about my hand, without even seeing it. Maybe he does see it.

Maybe I shouldn't, I think. *But what have I really got to lose?*

I yank off the glove, and watch as their mouths drop in awe.

"Think I know how your brother feels. I'm sorta in two places at once, myself. Except my mind is here, and my hand, I guess, is in the Realm."

"Okay . . . ," says Sula. "How did this happen exactly?"

"It's all in that mural up there."

I explain yesterday's mission to the Mercury, and how I found that box—the Magician's Lost and Found—and how my hand slipped inside.

As I talk, her eyes seem to see three times more than what I'm saying. I'm distracted by how pretty she is. Eyebrows thick like two perfect caterpillars, eyes round and big with eyelids heavy like a set of curtains in front of the whole universe, like if she opens them all the way you'll be lost in space.

"So you went to the theater looking for your dad?" Sula asks.

"Well, not exactly. Just hoping I'd find some clue about how to get him back."

"But King, *you made* a new breach. Remember, the

Realm is echoes of our world, copies made the moment there's a breach. The last breach before yesterday was four years ago, at the Mercury."

"How do you know that?" asks V.

"Because I *see* the Realm all the time, I know each echo pretty well by now. My brother is always painting them. *This* is the first new echo in four years." She points back up at the mural. That moment is looming over us in more ways than one.

"Okay," I say. "And that's a problem?"

"Don't you know how the Realm works?" she asks.

"I don't. Don't know what I'm doing. Feels like we covered this."

"Look, the Realm is made of echoes of our world, right? When you cause a rift, open a portal, whatever you want to call it, you start a new echo. But the old echoes are pushed back as soon as a new one is created. And eventually, you can't get back to those old echoes. They're out of reach from our reality. You follow me?"

"So you're saying . . ."

"That this place your dad's in—this echo, he may be stuck there forever soon. When you opened the Lost and Found, you put your dad's echo on the clock. Your dad—

and my dad and mom—are in that echo that's fading further away from our reality. It's only a matter of time. His echo could be lost in the Realm."

"Oh no," I say. "How long? How long do we have?"

Sol goes and digs through some piles of boards and canvas and comes back with a small dry-erase board attached to a chain, and a marker.

He writes on the board the number 13.

"Thirteen what?" I ask. "Thirteen hours? Thirteen days? What?"

He keeps on writing, another 13 below that.

"Look forward and backward, it's all the same," says Sula. "The Realm cycles in hours of thirteen. After two cycles"—she snaps her fingers—"time's up."

"WHAT TIME *WAS* it?" I realize that's the most important question. "What time was it when I found the box?"

I look from Too Tall to Veronica as if they might know the answer immediately.

They just shrug.

"I don't know, cuz," says V.

"Quick! We've got to figure it out!"

"Um, wait!" says Tall. "Why do we need to know that, exactly?"

I press my palms into my forehead.

"Because," Veronica says patiently. "When Kingston put his hand in the box, he made something happen in the

Realm. From that moment, we've got twenty-six hours—two cycles of thirteen—before his dad's echo is gone for good. At least, that's what I got."

I nod to her. "That's what I got, too."

We look to Sula. She nods. "Yes. I think that's right."

"Ah," says Tall. "Okay, let me think. What time was it? Phones keep time. And phones keep track of everything. Did we use any phones? Send any texts?"

I snap my fingers. "You made a note on your notepad, about the code."

"Yes!" Too Tall says, and thumbs through his phone. "That note was made . . . yesterday at 6:18 p.m."

"Okay, and then we wandered around that old theater for a while. Say I found the box, I don't know, twenty minutes later?"

"Call it 6:30, to be safe," says Veronica.

"Okay, so 6:30 p.m. yesterday plus twenty-six hours is—"

"It's 8:30 p.m. this evening," says V.

"Right. And the time now?" I ask.

"It's 5:03 p.m.," Tall reads from his phone.

Three hours . . .

"Hey, not so bad! Three whole hours!" says Too Tall.

I can't even tell if he's trying to be supportive or if he really thinks that's plenty of time. I just groan.

Three hours.

The thought makes me dizzy.

"So. What now?" he says.

"What now? I don't have the slightest idea! I don't have a clue how to make a portal or pull Dad through or even find Dad—I don't know!"

"Okay, big guy," says Tall. "I'm with ya. Take it easy now, I'm one of the good guys."

V puts a gentle hand on my shoulder.

"Right. Sorry," I say.

Sol writes something on the board where he'd written 13 twice. Only now, there's just one 13 written there. He takes the marker between the 1 and the 3 and draws a simple + sign.

"One plus three," says Veronica.

"Four," says Too Tall. "Right. Four."

"What's he mean?" I ask.

Sula shrugs.

"Great," says Too Tall. "More riddles and numbers. My favorite."

"Can you help us?" I ask Sula.

"Listen, I wish you good luck and all. But nothing

good happens when you mess with the Realm." Sol suddenly gives his sister a look. She reads his expression and nods. "Sol wants to help you, Kingston. But I don't know how to open a portal in the next three hours. I don't know how to open a portal at all, to tell you the truth. I know it's not easy, which is why no one has pulled it off in the last four years. I think there was some reason that my father had to open the portal when your dad was onstage. But to be completely honest, I'd rather Sol didn't go near the Realm, Urma, or anything having to do with any of it."

I nod when she's done talking. But my mind feels like the dome of the Mercury right now. Like there's a gaping hole in my skull and pigeons are flying in and out. I don't know what to do. Usually if I feel like this, I go to Mom. And if Mom's not there, I go to Dad. Well, not the real Dad, but the Dad Voice in my head. Even though Dad's been gone for years, I still can remember his voice so well that sometimes I can hear what he would say, even though he's not around to say it. Dad Voice would say something like, *Kid, you better look after that muralist,* or, *You better be nice to your mom and tell her the truth.*

It was always *you better*. But not like *you better do this or else*, it was more like *you better* be *a better you*. Pop was there to help me see how I could be better at being me.

But now I'm trying to hear what he would tell me to do, only it's not there. No Dad Voice. I close my eyes and listen, but there's nothing.

Like what will happen when his reality fades and he's gone for good.

"Whoa, King," says Veronica, seeing the dead look in my eyes. "Don't go too dark, now. Hang in there."

"What do we do, V?"

"Forgive me for suggesting this again, but don't you think it's time we talk to my dad?"

"You sure?"

"What's the worst he could do?"

"He could stop us," I say.

"Stop us from doing what?"

She's got me there.

Veronica goes on: "I'm just saying, we don't know what we're doing. And maybe my dad doesn't know about the fading echo. Maybe if we tell him, he'll want to help."

THE WALK BACK home takes exactly twelve minutes. Along the way, I think about how to tell Uncle Long Fingers everything we've been up to, from Urma Tan's hypnosis to Sol's painting of me. I wonder how much he already knows.

When we get home, I'm so ready to talk to Long Fingers that I'm actually shocked that my mother is the first person I see.

"Oh, hi, King!" she says.

She's sweaty in a tank top and her braids are pulled up in a high ponytail. She's hard at work clearing out the ground floor to turn the space into a café. She's made some progress. The walls are bare of any and all posters and signs of magic.

The shelving units are pushed to a wall. The velvet curtain that separated the front area is gone, and when you stand near the entrance, you can just about see all the way to the back room and the windows that look out on the backyard.

"Hi, Miss James!" says Too Tall.

"Welcome to the future King's Cup!" Ma returns his bright smile. "Would you all like a tour? Full disclosure, it may require some imagination."

"King's . . . Cup?" I repeat.

"You like it?" she asks with a wink.

"Well, yeah," I say.

"Okay, over here to my right," she says, and waves an open hand along the wall where the shelves are stacked, "will be the countertop. We'll serve the drinks here. We'll have all your milks and sugars and napkins and such. Behind that wall will be the kitchen. We're going to stain—yes, stain—this brick wall here. It'll be all nice and warm and red and exposed. Then here, here, there, and outside, this will all be seating areas . . ."

I start to zone out as Mom walks us through each part of her dream café. All I can think about is Pop. How can she stand there and yap away about this when we have *less than three hours* to save him?

Because she doesn't know, I remind myself. *Because you won't tell her.*

"King, are you okay?" she asks.

The seconds feel like an eternity as Too Tall, Veronica, and my mom all watch me.

Tell her, some voice urges from the back of my mind. *Tell her everything. She has a right to know.*

"I'm fine, Ma," I say.

"You don't like the name?"

"No, I love it. I appreciate it. Like, a lot."

"Okay. You don't sound too sure."

"Ma—I just need to talk to Uncle Long Fingers, really quick."

"Oh? That's so strange, because he just left."

"He *left*?" I almost shriek.

Mom shrugs. "I was as surprised as you. Him and Crooked Eye. They just took off. They wheeled this huge contraption out the back. Whole thing covered in a tarp. Wouldn't say where they were going, or when they're coming back. King, you sure you're okay?"

"It's just . . . this *game* we were going to play. Long Fingers, he had, like, the rules."

Mom looks at me like I have five heads. Then she scans

Veronica and Too Tall, who smile and nod like, *Exactly what King said.*

I'm so relieved when Ma finally nods back and goes to work. Not that I got away with anything. She'll ask later, why I'm acting so strange. But right now, we have under *three hours* and counting, and it looks like we'll have to try and pull something off without my uncle's help.

"He *left*?" Veronica says in amazement as we take the stairs up to the second floor. "Wow."

"What's so strange about that?" asks Too Tall.

"Nothing, if he were anyone else in the world," says V as we gather in the doorway to my room. "But my dad doesn't leave this place. Wild horses couldn't get him out the front door."

"Must be serious," I say.

"So what's the next move?" asks Tall.

"We got to hit Long Fingers's workshop," I say, ready to do just that. "Maybe we can figure out what he was building, and where he went or something." A plan is kicking into overdrive in my head. *And see if he left the Lost and Found behind.*

Because Urma came through a rift to the Realm. She knows how to do it.

And if I bring her the box, she will help me get him back.

The hard truth is, I would trade this box for my dad. Any day.

I lead the way through the doorway to the room with the wall of books.

"His lab is right back there. You'll like this, Tall. Watch this sick bookcase move," I say, and point to it. *"Whoops—"*

The book *The Four Elements of Magic* leans back on its spine and the wall rumbles and turns to reveal the opening passageway.

I'm standing about twelve feet away, looking at my Realm hand. Just by thinking about moving the book, I moved the book from across the room.

Too Tall covers his amazed mouth with his hands, like he saw a celebrity but knows it's not the time to shout their name.

I shrug. "I didn't mean to do that. I mean, I meant to go do that the normal way."

Finally he says, *"Ba-NA-nas."*

"I'd really like to understand the powers of that hand of yours better," says Veronica.

"Me too," I say.

Okay, I realize as I step into the passageway. *I'm moving books from across the room by accident.* My focus is so strong, it's almost out of my control. Glad Mom wasn't around to see that. I'd have some explaining to do.

My eyes adjust to the dim light and the red glow in the foyer. It's the old shrine to my father, with the pictures and clippings of him and his tricks. V reads the sign hanging over the doorway.

"*The Four Elements Open the Way.* Huh."

"What?" I ask.

"No, it's nothing. Just, four, like the number Sol showed us."

"*Four* Elements of Magic," I say.

"And these four walls here," she says.

I look from one wall to the next in the hexagonal room—six sides: one entrance, one exit, and four walls. "A wall for Dad's three best tricks . . . and one for the Mirror."

"Okay, that is a lot of fours. So what's it mean?" asks Too Tall, looming behind us in the tight space.

"I'm just thinking, those four elements, right? See, I know how my dad's mind works. *The Four Elements Open the Way.* Very clever. I bet you anything that's not about the book and this passageway. It's about the *actual* four elements, whatever those are."

"You mean like the four walls here?" asks Too Tall.

V smiles at me.

The pictures on each wall are each devoted to a different object. Three are of my dad's best-known tricks: Hooker's Vanishing Deck, the Skull of Balsamo, and William Tell's Pistol. The fourth wall is all pictures of Maestro's Mirror. Could each trick represent an element?

"The way these pictures are organized. It's no coincidence," I say. "Four tricks, four elements . . ."

Like Dad's book . . . More like the fourth member of our family . . .

Realizing there's one clue that's been right under our noses, I head back out the way we came.

"Where you going, King?" asks Tall.

"About time we checked out my dad's old book."

26

Back out at the wall of books, V removes *The Four Elements of Magic* from its wall contraption with a screwdriver from her dad's workshop.

The book is so old, pages are falling out as I leaf through. Tall bends to pick a couple off the floor.

I'm not gonna lie, the book is crazy hard to read. *F*s and *E*s are thrown into words in bizarre places, and some phrasing just sounds beyond odd. I stop at a passage that reads:

> *The third kinde of Magick containcth the whole Philofophy of Nature which bringeth to light the inmoft vertues, and extracleth them out of Natures hidden bofome to humane ufe;*

"Whoa," says Tall. "Is that even English?"

"It's Old English. Like old before spelling was a thing, I guess," says Veronica.

I keep paging through, searching for something I can understand. Then I stop at a page full of Dad's handwriting. "Here!" I say, and get a warm rush at the sight of the familiar script. Looping *L*s and bold *D*s in the handwriting that used to fill the pages of yellow legal pads stacked around the house.

"You can understand *that*?" says Tall.

"The Four Elements," I say as I decipher my dad's handwriting. "He's talking about the four elements. Just like the Magician's Lost and Found."

Tall looks at me, puzzled.

"The top of the box, it had the same *four* signs. The Pistol. The Deck of Cards. The Skull of Balsamo. And the Mirror."

"*The Four Elements Open the Way*," says Veronica. "Your dad was using three of them in his act every night."

"Yup. The William Tell's Pistol gag, Hooker's Vanishing Deck, and the Skull of Balsamo," I say excitedly. "Those were his go-tos."

"And Maestro's was the Mirror," Veronica says.

"It says here they each represent a different school of

magic, the Pistol is Force, the Cards are Illusion, the Skull is Mystic, and the Mirror is Sorcery."

"So they're like parts of a magic puzzle or something," Tall jumps in.

"Bingo," I say. "The box must bring the four elements together?"

Too Tall shrugs. "Maybe it's in the wood? Wish we had that thing. You think there's any chance your dad left the box in his workshop?"

"Only one way to find out," says Veronica. She has this determined look that makes me smile.

———

LONG FINGERS'S LAB looks very different without the man himself sitting in the middle of it all. I can actually see to the back wall without that big thing under the tarp in the middle. I look around, wondering how he and Crooked even got that thing out of here. There's some of the stuff from the magic store—the canes and mannequin hands—that my uncles stashed here. The taxidermy owls are high on a shelf, keeping watch. There's a bunch of blueprints tacked to the walls with handwriting scribbled all over them. There's a giant map of the world with dates scribbled across different places: Ancient Egypt, 2594 BC; Carthage, 146 BC; Ancient Rome, 44 BC; Britannia, 420; Paris, 1312; Florence, 1492; Edo, 1603; Budapest, 1881; West Africa, 1901; Louisville, 1934. There's a stack of mirrored shards. Each shard is cut in the shape of a lightning bolt. I find more and more of them as I look around for the box, all about the same size.

"He sure did leave in a hurry," Too Tall says, holding his hand to a warm coffee mug sitting on the desk.

"I don't see it here," I say. "Anyone?"

"Nothing," says V.

"Nada," says Tall.

"Hmm," I say. "Think Long Fingers took it with him?"

"Possible, I guess," says V. "Well, hey, look at that."

"What?" Tall and I say at the same time.

V runs her fingers alongside a cabinet about the size of a mini-fridge. The wood is stained blond and it has a five-pointed star tooled into the center of each side.

"My dad, he built this for me," she says.

"I'm all about a good trip down memory lane, but I think we're on the clock here," Tall says.

V ignores him and traces her finger along the five-pointed star.

"A five-sided star is also five *V*s joined together." She

bends to pull the cabinet away from the wall. "*Whoa*, this thing got heavy," she says as she turns it around.

The side she reveals has a metal latch and lock bolted to it. There's a four-digit number combination beside the lock.

Tall face-palms. "I mean enough already, it's like this family does everything in code."

V starts playing with the combination.

"You think you can figure it out?" I ask.

"Like I said, I know how my dad's mind works," she says, turns the last number wheel, and unlatches the lock. She opens the lid of the cabinet and it releases air with a hiss. "Five *V*s. Or, five fives. In other words, five to the fifth power," V explains. "Five to the fifth power equals 3,125." She shrugs. "That's the code: 3125."

The inside of the cabinet is lined with steel chrome, like a real safe.

There at the bottom, looking like a buried treasure, is the Magician's Lost and Found.

"Why you smiling like that?" Tall asks V.

"No, it's nothing. He knows that I would guess that code. Didn't know he trusted me like that."

"I'm so glad he did," I say, and pick up the Lost and Found.

The Watch of 13 is even still in the locking mechanism. I notice the watch hand is on the 11. Are the watch hands clicking toward Dad's fading echo? I look at my own watch. It's 6:25 p.m.; we're about two hours away from the 13.

"What, King?" asks V.

"Two hours and counting," I say, and open up the Lost and Found, hoping for a clue, some direction, anything to help get Pops back before it's too late.

There's a handwritten note floating near the top. I'd know that handwriting anywhere.

It's my dad's.

THIS NOTE WASN'T here before. He wrote this. Recently.

Not four years ago, gathering dust.

He wrote this now. Like, in the present. He's alive, he has a hand, and that hand held a pen and wrote this note. And now it's in my hands.

I realize this is the closest I've been to my dad in nearly four years.

Tall prods, "What's it say?" like he can't take the suspense anymore.

I read it to them:

"Message received, big brother. Will be at appointed place by thirteenth hour. The elements await you in Black

Herman's grave, but you'll have to pull a Henry Brown to get them."

In the silence that follows, I read the words over and over again.

"Wow," says V. "That's a lot."

"Yeah," I agree.

"So the note was meant for my father?" she observes.

"Apparently," I say.

"It sounds like my dad is trying to save your dad after all, huh?"

"Yeah, I think so."

She leans in to read the note herself. "What's this, 'appointed place'?"

"I have no idea. Must be something they worked out between the two of them." Still, something about all of this is bothering me.

"King, why do you sound so glum? Isn't this good news?"

"I dunno, V. It's just, we're running out of time, and Long Fingers didn't even see this note yet, obviously. You see this reference to Black Herman's grave?"

"I did notice that," says V.

"Tall, is there a graveyard in Echo City?"

"Not that I know of."

"I thought so." I dig in my shorts pocket for the map and lay it out. "I'm pretty sure I remember seeing some sort of grave reference on here . . . *There.* Look," I say, and point to a spot on the map by Algernon Lane and Broken Jade Junction. *Graveyard Gate*, it says. "I'm going." I start packing up the map.

"Whoa, whoa, King, not so fast," says V.

I turn on a dime. "*Yes*, so fast. Matter-of-fact, not nearly fast enough. The clock is ticking, V. We don't even know what we're doing or whether we're on the right track. But I got to try something. And this makes the most sense. Come or stay, but I'm going."

I stop at my room to strap on my backpack after I slide the Lost and Found inside and zip up. Then I lead the way back downstairs and to the front door as quickly as possible.

"Leaving us already?" My mom intercepts us. She has a rag in hand like she's just scrubbed all of Echo City by herself. She can't seem to decide whether to be concerned or playful.

"Um, yeah, Ma, it's that game we were playing," I say.

"The one that Uncle Long Fingers knows the rules to?" asks Mom, eyes squinted in suspicion.

"Yeah. That one. And it's like, we got to go back outside . . ."

"Outside, huh? Well, that sounds nice. I was going to ask if you wanted to go for a walk, I haven't been out all day," says Ma.

"Um, well, the thing is . . ." I'm trying to think of a reason she can't come, but I'm coming up blank.

My hesitation isn't lost on Ma. "Are you ducking me, King?" she asks.

"No, Ma, I swear."

"I'm only kidding," she says, and then tilts her head. "Sorta."

"Let's spend time together tomorrow, okay, Ma? Tomorrow, I promise, I'll help out with the house and everything. All day, I'm here."

Maybe with Pop, I think. *Maybe we'll all be here and we can get back all that lost time.*

"Okay," she says. "Veronica, you're playing this game, too?"

"Sure am, Auntie," she says. "Tons of fun."

"Okay. Well, don't have too much fun. Keep an eye on King, V. Please, for me. King's not exactly used to the big city these days. Don't let him get too carried away."

Veronica pauses awkwardly. "I—I won't let him. I

mean, I'll keep both eyes on him, Auntie. Not to worry."

"I'll try not to. Good to see you, Eddie. See you later, King. Love you."

"See you, Ma."

As soon as she nods, we're out the door.

It isn't until I take the steps down to the sidewalk that I realize I didn't say *I love you* back.

———————————

THE SHADOWS FALL heavy and stretch long on the sidewalk as time inches closer to the thirteenth hour.

"So tell me, what's up with the rest of that note?" Tall asks me.

"Which part?"

"Well, whose grave are we going to, for one?"

"Black Herman," says Veronica. "Famous old magician from back in the day. He was like a hero to our dads."

"Oh yeah, you mentioned him yesterday. He was the one that would fake his own death and come back?"

"He had this old saying," I explain. "*The Great Black Herman Returns Every Seven Years.* Had it printed on all his old posters and everything."

Veronica says, "Yeah, he'd, like, bury himself alive, and days later be dug up. Then he'd lead a crowd to the local theater and do a show."

"Okay, not bad," says Tall. "Think he'd charge for the burial and the show, like, sell two separate tickets?"

Veronica scoffs. "Probably. In between, he'd even go to nearby towns and be buried alive there, too. Then he'd just keep it going. He'd tour the whole country. Think that was the deal with the whole *Returns Every Seven Years* thing. Took a while to get around back then."

"Sure, maybe that's it," I say. "But everything we learned about magic, we learned before we knew that magic was real. Maybe those stories aren't so straightforward."

"You think he really died and came back to life?" V says with a sarcastic grin.

"I'm just saying, we don't know anything, for real. I mean, was he from Virginia, like history says? Or was he born in a town in West Africa, like his book says?"

"Um, I'm gonna go with what history says, King," says V with a chuckle. "That book is full of nonsense so he could make money. Like you really think he went to Egypt, India, China, and Paris? *Pfft.* If there was anything magic about that guy, it was how he could turn a profit. Even after he died, they sold tickets to see his body."

"Well, he faked his death for most of his career. No one believed it when he actually died."

Too Tall nods, impressed. "You two really know a lot about this guy, huh?"

"Sure," says V. "In a house like ours, full of Black magicians? Black Herman is like the Black Houdini, only no one's heard of him."

"He was a good man, too, Tall. He supported his community. He'd give loans to Black businesses, scholarships to students, and do free performances to help struggling churches. He never turned his back on his people."

"And what was the other name on there?" asks Tall.

This one I'm less sure about. "It was Henry Brown. Some old magician, I guess. Don't remember his act."

"Henry 'Box' Brown," says Veronica. "Was a slave, in Virginia. He mailed himself north, to Philadelphia, and freedom." She taps my backpack, knuckle rapping the wood of the Magician's Lost and Found. "In a small wooden box."

We walk in silence for a while, and I wonder if this small wooden box can help free my pops, wherever he may be.

Turns out "Graveyard Gate" isn't a graveyard, exactly, but a mural of one. The painting runs half the length of an Echo City block on the forgotten wall of an abandoned car wash. There's a ladder propped up against the wall. Sol is standing toward the top of the ladder, painting something.

Veronica, Too Tall, and I shrug all at once. Sol doesn't seem to notice us, and we don't want to disturb him. He's so focused on his craft, it feels wrong.

We take in the mural. The painted gates are the first thing I notice. The bars are black and high, curling into spirals at the top. There's a hill at the center of the mural and there's a mausoleum at the summit. Sol is painting something inside the mausoleum. Something very small that I can't see.

Gravestones line the way along the sloping hill. Some stand tall and proud with names and phrases declared in bold letters, but none I can actually read. Some are small like rocks, and a couple are made of wood. I try to get close enough to read the names, but the closer I get, the less sense the letters make, like trying to read in a dream.

Sol slides down the ladder with ease and looks at us like he knew we were there all this time.

"Hey, Sol. Where's your sister?" I ask.

He has his dry-erase board hanging on a chain around his neck. He writes something in marker:

The more you look the less you see.

"This kid sure is expert with the cryptic scribbles," says Too Tall, reading the board.

Sol just looks at me and nods, like it all makes perfect sense.

"He's *amazing*," says Veronica, gazing at the graveyard mural with awe. "How long did this take you?"

Sol shrugs.

He's looking at my backpack now with that eerie glare of his. He touches the box through the canvas.

"Um, yeah," I say, very confused. What do I tell him? I

think he's trying to help me. In fact, I'm pretty sure if Sula had her way, he wouldn't be here with us now.

"I've got the Lost and Found," I tell him.

The kid's eyes go round and wide and he nods.

"You want me to take it out?"

He nods some more.

I take the Lost and Found out of my backpack. I open it up, check around the edges, and press against the felt lining. There's nothing there.

Sol's eyes widen when he sees the box. I let him hold it.

I point to the mural. "Which one of these is Black Herman's grave?" I ask him.

He glances at me, and then returns his attention to the box like I never said a word. He runs his fingers around its edges carefully, like he's memorizing every detail.

"Hey," I say, pointing to a stone in the mural. "You painted these, right? Well, I can't read the names on the gravestones. Which one is Black Herman's?"

Not that I'd have a clue what to do next.

He takes me by the hand and steps up to the graveyard gates. He takes the box and sets it against where the handle is painted.

"You want me to put my hand in there?" I ask.

"Oh, you've got to be kidding me," says Veronica.

Sol shakes his head.

"That kid don't look like he's joking," says Tall.

Sol waves me to come closer, and nods in a way that says, *It's okay. Trust me.*

I let him take me by the wrist of my gloved hand and guide it toward the box.

"Okay, I think I get it," I say.

I open the lid of the box and feel a waft of cold air.

Then he tugs the fabric of my white glove and shakes his head.

"No good?" I ask.

He shakes his head some more.

"Sure thing, I gotcha." I take off the glove.

I'm still not quite used to having no visible hand. Even as I wiggle my invisible fingers, I expect to see them.

Sol's smile is full of tiny teeth. He sets his feet and holds the box steady like a catcher who just called a pitch.

I reach my hand through the box.

And my hand keeps going. Past the bottom of the box, past where the wall should be, until I feel the hard metal of a handle in my palm, cool to the touch.

My expression must be crazy because Sol just smiles at me like, *See?*

He nods.

Keep going.

My heart is beating a million miles an hour. There's no visible explanation for what's happening. My hand is *through the box* and *through the wall* somehow.

And now I'm holding the handle to a painted gate, and the handle is cool and hard as iron.

I turn the handle and feel its rusty creak.

Nervous laughter bursts through my teeth.

There's a rush of cold air.

"This is *ama—*"

Fog consumes me. Thick, gushing fog that fills my mouth and throat and surprises the breath out of me. I'm blinded by the cool gray like I've just walked into a cloud.

"V? Tall?" I say, but my voice is muffled by the fog. "Hello? Sol? Anyone?" But the words bounce right back.

The fog clears in front of me. I see the bars of the gates to the graveyard. The handle is still in my hand. But the painted grass behind it is . . . *actual* grass.

Where in holy Houdini am I?

I PUSH THE gate open and the metal scrapes the earth. My heart is pounding so hard it rattles my chest. I look behind me, but there's a wall of fog so thick it might as well be made of cement. Veronica, Tall, and Sol are gone.

It's just me, the graveyard, and the box.

I let go of the handle once I'm in the gates, and I take the box in both hands and press it close to my chest. I'm hoping it'll keep the bad things away.

When I look down, I notice something shocking.

I have *two* visible hands.

Amazed, I hold my left hand up in front of me. I take in every little detail, every line in my palm.

Where am I? I wonder again. *Am I in the Realm?*

Seems there's nowhere to go but forward, so that's where I go. One step after the next in the chilly, wet grass.

A shiver runs down my spine, and it's not just from wearing short sleeves in the sudden cold. It's the blackout darkness of the sky. The fog breaking like waves over the edges of gravestones. The stone monuments and statues of people in frock coats with blank eyes. The brambles and bushes cluttered on top of one another.

"The more you look the less you see," I hum to myself.

I stop at each stone to look at the names. I can read them now. One stone slab that's half buried in fallen leaves reads, *Doctor Peter*. Next to that are a few prickly plants, like cedars and yuccas. A collection of seashells marks another grave. Some graves are marked by workers' objects like an iron pipe and a slab of maybe railroad iron. There's a large statue of a man, carved head to toe in dark bronze. He's wearing a tuxedo jacket with tails and a bow tie and he's holding a skull in his hands. He stands on a platform with the words *In Memory of the Celebrated Ventriloquist Who Died Sept. 20, 1825.* I realize it's Richard Potter, America's first Black magician.

"He wasn't just the first Black magician, you know," says a voice.

"Who's there?"

I snap my head right and left, up and down, my heart racing.

But I don't see anyone.

"He was America's first *magician*, full stop," the voice continues.

"Who's talking?" I say, my own voice shaking. "Come out!"

"Oh. Sorry. Wait for it," he says—I can't see him yet, but I'm pretty sure it's a he. His voice wobbles like a preacher-performer.

The black clouds drift apart and a moonbeam cuts through the darkness.

A man emerges in the moonbeam like a spotlight. He's like a sketch, only half drawn. He's made up of shades and shadows and empty space and pale light. He smiles and winks like he made the clouds move and the moon shine all by himself. He's tall and handsome, and he wears a pyramid-shaped medallion and a Prince Albert coat.

"You . . . *you're*—no, it's not possible."

"Ah, but my boy, I specialize in the impossible."

"I saw you. Back at the Mercury. That was you, wasn't it?"

"Indeed it was."

I can see his face clearer than ever before. He looks just like he does in the old magic posters.

"You're Black Herman," I say.

He grins as though he's pleased to be recognized. "I go by a lot of names. I'm most proud of the Great Black Herman, Master of Legerdemain."

I blink and blink to adjust to the strange way he appears in the moonlight, like a hologram of a black-and-white photo. As he moves, some parts of him vanish, like the outline of his strong jawline, or the lapels of his coat. The parts of him that would be in shadow just simply aren't there. "But what happened to the rest of you?" I ask him. "Are you some kinda ghost?"

"Not exactly. But I don't mind if you call me a ghost, if a ghost is how you see me. But I never did die. At least, not in the normal sense. I took too many trips to the Realm. Just didn't quite make it back in one piece."

"I don't understand. Are we in the Realm?"

"Well, I'm not sure *we* are anywhere."

"What do you mean? Is this the Realm?" I ask.

"My own little corner of it, yes."

"I thought the Realm was just echoes of reality."

"There are so many little realms in what we call the Realm. Most of them are echoes. 'Cause the folks that made them didn't have any idea what they was doing. But young man, I am the Master of Legerdemain and this here is my own little realm within the Realm, gloomy though it may be. I made this. And I made it to my liking."

"You . . . *made* this place?"

"That I did. Welcome to 'Black Herman's Private Graveyard.' A place for all us Black magicians to rest. Honor us the way we'd want to be honored—each in our own way. Those plants right there are for the old Obeah doctors and healers, straight from West Africa. You see Richard Potter got himself a nice fancy statue—he did well for himself, so he got a right to enjoy it. That there is Isaac Willis—the Great Boomsky—"

I see where he's pointing and look at the gravestone. The letters read:

The More You Look the Less You See.

So *that's* why Sol wrote those words when I was trying to read the stones on the mural.

"This one here is Professor J. Herman Moore, the Prince of Mystery. Did you know I was—"

"His assistant?"

Black Herman smiles and looks astonished.

I nod and play it cool. Not every day you surprise a two-hundred-year-old legendary ghost. Or Realm spirit. Or whatever he is.

"Well, I'll be. Didn't think folks still spoke about me nowadays."

"My dad told me all about you. You're his hero."

"Well, heroes are funny things. Wait a minute," he says, and drifts closer, examining me. "Heh, well, look at that. You favor him, you know. I know your dad. He came here."

"He did?" I nearly shriek.

"He sure did. More than once. In fact, last visit he paid me was just a short while ago."

"So I just missed him?"

"Only just."

"Wait, so if he walked in here, and I walked in here, can't he come back and meet me? Can't he just leave with me?"

"Leave with you?" Black Herman repeats with a hefty chuckle. "Son, what makes you think you're actually *here*?"

"What do you mean?"

"Hate to break it to you, but you are not, as it were, here."

"I'm not here? But you're like a ghost—you're not here!"

"Far as I can tell, I am here for the foreseeable. No, if you really were in this place, you'd have a heck of a time getting back. Look for yourself. You cast a shadow?"

I look down and realize no, there's no shadow at all. I wave my hand in the moonlight and look at where it strikes the grass, but there's nothing.

"Then how can you be here, if you don't cast a shadow?" he asks.

"But I feel the cold," I say, wondering how this is possible, how I could be here but not here. "The wet grass and the rocky ground."

"The mind is a powerful trickster. To me, you're about as real as I am to you."

"So I'm imagining all of this?"

"It's a bit more complicated than that. You must have seen this place somewhere in your world, am I right? It's about reflections and gates."

"Reflections?"

"Yeah. That's how I discovered the Realm for the first time. Your pops, too. Reflections are magic, young man."

"They make the world into more worlds," I say.

"Quite handsomely put."

"My friend painted this graveyard. It was a huge mural. That's how I found it."

"Interesting. Your friend can bring reflections to life, then. I saw my first glimpse of the Realm in a stained-glass window in a small church in Louisville. Your father told me he saw this graveyard in a reflection in a pool of rainwater by a gutter when Brooklyn got flooded one time."

"And I saw you in the reflection in the glass at the Mercury," I say, realizing I actually saw the Realm without realizing.

"I suppose so. But actually, physically being here? That's something different. First time your daddy came, he was dream-visiting, just like you. Eventually, he figured out how to receive some gifts I left for him. This last visit, he came for real. Rode the echoes and showed up in person. Imagine my surprise when he returned those gifts for safekeeping." I remember the note Pops left for Long Fingers. *The elements await you in Black Herman's grave.* The "gifts" Black Herman is talking about must be the elements. "He left them somewhere—those gifts?"

"He did," Black Herman says with a cryptic look. "What brings *you* here?"

"My dad. I'm here to find my dad. To bring him back home."

He looks me up and down. "Some folks aren't meant to walk in just one world."

"But if he can walk into your world, he can walk back into mine."

He grins like I'm not quite following him. "I wasn't talking about your daddy."

"Me?"

"You got the look. You got faraway lands on the mind. And you're ready and willing to go places, no matter what the risk."

"I'm just here 'cause I want to find my pops."

"Sure, that's how it starts. Then you find you need to keep moving. Being in one world don't feel quite right. You start to feel stuck. You know the places you dream about be real and that knowledge be calling to you. Next thing you know, you riding echoes."

"Riding echoes?"

"That's how you get from place to place in the Realm. That's how I was born in Virginia. Then it was the jungles of West Africa. Then I made it to Egypt. India. 'Cause each trip was like I was born again."

"*The Great Black Herman Returns Every Seven Years,*" I say.

"That's right. I used to say that at every show. I'd always find my way back, you see. I set this place to give me someplace to go once I was done with it all. Faked my death one last time, and slipped out here. I let the clock run out, the portal shut, and now I don't leave here, not anymore."

"Wow," I say, thinking about how Dad might get trapped in his echo. "That sounds rough."

"It's not so bad. I was tired of running myself down, hopping from echo to echo. I miss performing sometimes. The crowds. And I miss jumping from world to world, across oceans and eras. Would you believe I visited the pharaoh's court in Egypt, met history's first magician, Dedi himself, almost five thousand years ago? Nah, you probably wouldn't believe that. But it's true. And come to find out, he wasn't the first by a long shot. In fact, we lucky to even know his name."

"Wait, so you traveled back *in time*?"

"Well, sort of. As you said, the Realm is full of echoes. Each one is a moment in time, preserved. And you can jump from one echo to the next, if you know how to do it."

"But I thought once the rift closes, you can't leave your echo anymore."

"Well, that's not quite the case. See, each echo is a twenty-six-hour loop of a moment in time. A moment centered around—"

"A rift," I say.

"Correct. Now, everything about that echo stays the same as the moment in real time, including the rift. So at the thirteenth hour, there's a rift somewhere in each echo, and if you can find it, you can jump through it, into other echoes. We call it riding echoes. But it's a dangerous pastime, young man, and you could end up stuck."

"How do you end up stuck?"

"When you ride echoes, you can miss and get stuck in the portal itself. You have to be careful."

"Mr. Herman, I'm not trying to ride echoes or anything like that. I lost my pop. I just want him back."

"But your daddy's not the type to sit still. You might have to follow him."

"I need to open a portal or a gate or something, just to pull him through before it's too late. He's coming home. I know he is. He just needs my help."

"You might be right about that. If you can open a portal, and he meets you there, you should be able to help him home, as long as there's no new echo pushing your daddy's echo out of reach. But opening a portal—that ain't exactly child's play."

"You need the four elements of magic. Right? Force, Illusion, Mystic, and Sorcery. That's how you open a portal, when all four elements come together. Right?" I ask, though I can't picture how this might work.

"Heh. Quite the magic student we got here. Well, your

daddy got three of them from me, anyway. My three best tricks. He must have got the fourth from somewhere else."

He sure did. Maestro's Mirror.

"Where?" I ask.

"I couldn't say."

"No, I mean did he get the objects from your grave?"

"You make your own daddy sound like a common grave robber. Yes, he got them from me, but he had my blessing. We talked, just like you and me are doing. And I showed him the way."

"And that's where he returned them?"

Black Herman shows a sly grin.

"Please. Show me the way."

He turns his head to the mausoleum up on top of the hill.

He winks and smiles. The clouds move and the moonlight fades and the half-lit sketch of Black Herman vanishes into the shade.

THE MAUSOLEUM IS dedicated to the life of Black Herman. Scenes of his greatest triumphs are carved in stone along the walls. There's him at a stadium of thousands. Him in his study in Harlem, surrounded by well-dressed community folks. Him at the pharaoh's court in ancient Egypt. Him as a young man in a small West African town. Him in a coffin, buried alive before a crowd in America.

There's a familiar box that's set on a podium against the back wall.

I look at the box in my hands, to make sure it's still there.

The Lost and Found and the box against the wall are practically identical. The only difference I can see is the locking mechanism with the Watch of 13. The box in Black Herman's mausoleum doesn't have one. Otherwise, they are the same.

I reach to open Black Herman's box, but my hand goes right through. I try again, but it's like the box is only an illusion.

"That won't work. *You* not here, my boy."

I look around for Black Herman, but don't see him. It's just his voice talking to me.

"So how do I get the elements?" I ask, getting an anxious chill.

"The box, young man. The place where the fading echo meets the rising earth."

"What? That's just a riddle," I say. "Give me something I can do."

"Your daddy figured it out."

That makes me pause.

If my dad figured it out, so can I.

Black Herman must have known that would work on me. Am I that easy to see through?

The box, the box . . .

Where the fading echo meets the rising earth.

I don't know what that means. But I do know there's two boxes, one a Realm box and one a real box (though at this point I don't know which is which).

If I'm looking for the place where they meet, maybe I should introduce them to each other?

I set the box in my hands over the top of the box on the platform.

"That's it," Black Herman says.

I line up the sides of each box so there's no space between the two. I lower the Lost and Found box so it phases *through* the podium box. When the two boxes occupy the exact same space, I hold still. To my naked eye, it looks like one single box.

Only I'm afraid of what's going to happen if I let go. Will the Lost and Found keep phasing and fall through the podium and through the floor? If none of this is really here, what is there to hold it up?

I close my eyes. *Trust,* I think. *This is the spot where the fading echo meets the rising earth.*

It has to be.

I let go of the box and open my eyes.

The Lost and Found sits on top of the podium in Black Herman's mausoleum. Two boxes are now one.

I touch the wood and it feels solid, too. I open the lid, reach in, and pull out a leather sack tied with leather strings.

One by one, I remove the objects.

The deck of cards.

The pistol.

The skull.

And a shard of mirror glass in the shape of a lightning bolt.

A smile spreads across my face.

I got you, Dad. I'm coming.

I CARRY THE Lost and Found back down the hill, heavy with the four objects rattling around inside.

Getting closer, I think, hurrying to the gates. *Closer to Dad, closer to—*

Then I stop short.

I realize I don't know what's the *appointed spot,* according to Dad and Long Fingers. I don't know where to go next. Assuming I can get out of this graveyard. Which I'm hoping won't be a problem—according to Black Herman, I never left Echo City. Only my mind is here. Or something.

"Black Herman?" I say just before the tall gates.

I look around. I hope he hears me.

"If you were going to go back to reality from the Realm, where would you do it?" I ask him.

There's a moment of quiet, and then Herman says, "I'm disappointed, Kingston. I thought you could figure that out on your own. When I performed my buried-alive trick, where would I return?"

I grin. "The same spot where you left. Got it, Black Herman. Thank you for all of your help. It was a great honor meeting you. I'll never forget it. Hope to see you again, somehow."

I open the gates and step through, toward the heavy fog.

I'm waiting for something to happen, but nothing does.

"Ahem," says Black Herman.

I think for a moment.

The same spot where you left . . .

"Okay, okay, I think I get it," I say.

I close the gate behind me and turn the handle with a squeaky *clang*.

I get a rush of warmth as the fog consumes me once more. My vision goes blank and there's a sound like when you cup your ear to seashells. The world starts spinning. I have to close my eyes to keep from getting dizzy . . .

I open them, and I'm at the mural of the graveyard. I'm holding the Lost and Found against the wall.

But I lose my balance and fall to the sidewalk and drop the box.

"King!" I hear the combined voices of Veronica and Too Tall.

I roll onto my back and look up.

There are three faces. My cousin looks like she might actually cry. Tall's eyes are wide. Only Sol seems pretty cool about everything.

"What happened, King? Are you okay? Please tell me you're okay," says Veronica.

"I think so, V," I say, rubbing my forehead and feeling the concrete against the back of my head like rock-hard sandpaper.

"Good," she says, recovering. "Because your mom will kill me. And that won't work for me, I like living."

"Can you get up?" asks Tall. "Or you need to lay there for a bit?"

"I'm up, I'm up," I say as though talking to an alarm clock that's gone off too many times.

I hold out my left hand for Tall to take it and help me up.

I realize my hand is gone once again. I should be

used to it by now, but after having it back, it takes me a second. *How did I have it back just now?* I wonder. *Was it real?*

Did I ever have it back? Or was that just my mind, being tricky with me?

"King? King! You there?" asks Tall. "How hard did you hit your head?"

"Tall, how long was I gone just now?"

"What do you mean, *how long were you gone*?" asks Too Tall.

I open my mouth to clarify, but something stops me. I try to imagine everything that's happening from Tall and V's perspective, and I realize I can't. I have no idea what the last few moments looked like to them.

"What did you see me do, just now?" I ask. "You saw me turn the handle through the box, right?"

"You stuck your hand through," says V, "and turned your wrist. Then you made a dreamy face. Then you turned your hand again, dropped the box, and collapsed."

So that whole trip to the graveyard happened in a fraction of time. My body never actually left, like Black Herman said.

The box—I think in a panic—*the four objects!*

I rush to where I dropped the box on the sidewalk.

It lies on its side. I turn the box upright and open it with shaking hands.

"What's *that*?" asks Tall.

The leather bag is still there.

Whew.

"I get that this sounds crazy," I say. "But just now, I was *in that graveyard.*"

Sol starts chuckling.

"What's so funny, little man?" Too Tall asks with some bass in his voice.

"Listen to me. *I'm* telling you, it's true."

I explain to them about the enchanted graveyard of magic Black America, and how I met Black Herman in a Prince Albert coat, and how I saw him in a reflection before.

They're listening carefully to every word. Though I can't tell if they believe me.

So I pull out the leather bag and untie the leather strings.

"Here. I found this in the graveyard, just like Dad's note said."

I take out the Skull of Balsamo—a preserved human skull with copper lining the jawbone. That gets a *wow* out of them. Then Hooker's Vanishing Deck—looks like an ordinary deck of cards, with a bear-head insignia. Then William Tell's Pistol, an old-timey six-shooter with a long barrel. And then the shard of mirrored glass.

Too Tall and V look stunned.

"We have the four elements. You understand now?" I say.

"This is unbelievable, King," Veronica says, holding up the copper-lined skull and looking in its blank eye sockets.

"I know. I mean, thanks. I mean, what time is it? We got to go."

"Where to?" asks Tall.

"When you want to return to reality from the Realm, you got to come back the way you came."

THERE'S A U-HAUL truck parked behind the Mercury. The loading entrance to the theater is actually open, and the truck is wedged into the dock at an odd angle. Whoever left this here was in a hurry. We walk around the truck, and the loading entrance takes us through a tunnel and backstage.

One thing hasn't changed—the Mercury is so quiet you can hear your own heartbeat.

I check the Watch of 13 lodged in the Lost and Found. The hour hand is just past the 12 and creeping toward the thirteenth hour. One more turn of the small hand and I may never see him again.

"What time you got?" I ask V.

"7:32." She glances at the watch on her wrist. "Fifty-eight minutes, scratch that, fifty-seven. 7:33 now."

Too Tall, Veronica, Sol, and I look out from stage left.

On the stage, there's a huge object with a tarp draped over it, about seven feet tall. It's the same behemoth that Long Fingers had in his workshop. Now it stands right on top of the trapdoor where I found the Lost and Found to begin with.

"Well, I'm guessing my dad and uncle brought that thing in the U-Haul, huh? But where are they?" says Veronica.

"*Hello!*" I call, my voice bouncing around the old theater. "Uncle Crooked Eye? Uncle Long Fingers?"

No response.

But it does feel good to hear my own voice echo back to me. Like I've announced myself to all the phantom shows and crowds that linger in this magic-rich place.

I'm here. And I've come to bring Dad home.

We approach the tarp on center stage.

"What do you suppose it is?" asks Too Tall.

"I think I know," I say.

"Wait, King," says Veronica. "This is super creepy. Where are my dad and Uncle Crooked?"

I shrug. "I'm sure they're just on the way to the graveyard and we missed them."

"But won't they need the Lost and Found to go to the graveyard? I'm telling you, King, this is suspect," V says.

"Look, we have the box, and the elements. We can't waste any more time."

I take the tarp in hand and give it a pull with a flourish to reveal the Mirror.

"I knew it!" I say. "This is what he was working on. Your dad wanted to get his brother back just as much as I did."

Sol steps forward and stares up at the Mirror.

"Whoa," says Tall. "You mean your uncle *made* this?"

"Right under our noses," I say, and admire the craftmanship. It's an exact replica of Maestro's Mirror, right down to the snakes tooled into the wood and meeting at the very top. The only missing part is a lightning-shaped hole in the center of the glass.

"Uncle Long never gave up on Dad, though the whole world thought he did," I say, taking out one object from the Lost and Found at a time and setting them down in front of the Mirror. The skull. The cards. The pistol.

"I was wondering where the glass had gone, after the fire. It was your dad, V. He came and gathered up all the glass he could."

I take the last object out of the bag. The lightning-shaped mirror shard.

"So *that's* why all those shards in his workshop," says V.

"Yup. That shard must have gone through to the other side with Dad. At his workshop, we saw how he tried to duplicate the glass, but it needed this piece to work, all along. Dad had to pass it back. Long Fingers needed the Lost and Found."

"But King, don't you think it's a little sketch that this Mirror is just waiting here like this?"

I lower the lid of the box and I check the Watch of 13 as it ticks toward the 13.

"We're running out of time, V."

Sol points to the hole in the Mirror. He nods to me. With trembling fingers, I set the lightning-bolt-shaped shard into the empty space in the Mirror like the last piece of a jigsaw puzzle.

"Okay, what happens now?" asks Tall. "Don't you need some Gorilla Glue or something so it holds?"

He gets his answer as something clicks. Blue light

starts blazing from all four objects. The skull glows with blue in its eyes. The cards look like they're surrounded by blue flame. The pistol has a blue flame streaming from the nozzle. And a blue star appears in the depths of the Mirror.

And then it expands like a rising blue sun, pushing away our reflection.

A silhouette is in front of the blue light.

The tall shape of a man.

A figure I know so well.

He steps forward and the blinding blue recedes behind him. His features become clear. Double-dimpled smile. Salt-and-pepper stubble. The same black suit he wore the night of his last performance.

He keeps moving forward. Toward me. Toward us.

He smiles. His eyes narrow.

His open hand reaches for me, and I reach back with my Realm hand.

We did it, I think, *he's here!*

It's just me and Dad.

I forget everything else. I don't even know where the glass ends and he begins. I don't know whether I'm standing onstage or I'm inside the Mirror.

All I know is we clasp hands. His grip is strong.

His eyes smile and tear with relief. He mouths, *King*.

Then something happens. There's a loud shout. I hear my name, I think.

But I don't look away. I won't. I hold on . . .

There's an arm wrapped around me. Another arm that hooks my right elbow as a hand lands on my chest.

"Kingston, no!"

It's *Mom*.

I **REALIZE MOM** doesn't even *see* Pop.

I'm half inside the Mirror. She's holding me from center stage. I grip Pop's hand with my Realm hand. Mom is pulling us both back toward her. She's trying to rescue me from the Mirror. But she's actually helping me bring Dad back home.

Then there's an eruption of blue light.

Ferocious energy floods in on me like a dam broke somewhere within the Mirror. There's so much force I lose my grip and Pop's hand slips away.

No—

Something's horribly wrong.

Blue light blasts from the Mirror. I don't see Pops anymore. Tons of light and energy pour into our world.

I tumble back out of the Mirror and onto the stage floor. Mom falls with me, clutching me to her chest.

Mom gets to her feet, still clutching me. "What are you doing, King? Are you trying to toss yourself away, just like he did?"

I feel her nails bite my arm. Her hands are trembling and it's like they send an electric current through me, shaking me. "He was here," I blubber. "I had his hand in my hand, Mom! We can bring him back!"

But she doesn't hear me at all. She gets to her knees, ignoring me and the blazing blue light rushing from the Mirror. "And if this young lady hadn't come looking for her little brother, what would have happened then, Kingston?"

I notice Sula is behind her. She's got her arm around Sol, who's shaking her off like he's seriously annoyed and pointing up to the roof.

A burst of wind crashes down from above. Cold air fills the warm, humid theater as overhead beams buckle and crack.

I look to the hole in the roof. The light from the Mirror surges up there.

A voice booms. It's deep and carries through the entire place.

"The night the caterpillar's world ends . . ."

A figure floats down from the hole in the roof, spotlit by the intense beam of blue light-energy.

It's Urma Tan, gliding through the rafters, head to toe in black with crystals woven throughout her dress.

"The night the caterpillar's world ends," she says in her smooth, prowling voice, "the caterpillar sees darkness. But something much more beautiful emerges."

She looks alive. Power radiates off her as she descends from above.

The light in the Mirror is like a blazing star. I have to squint to see that Pop . . . is gone.

Mom turns to Urma. "What in the world?"

Urma drifts and hovers just a few feet above the stage. She holds out a gloved hand toward the Mirror. The blue star leaps from inside the glass and levitates to her fingertips as though she called it to her. She tilts her head back, opens her mouth, and eases the star down her throat. She glows from the inside. The blue energy beams through her translucent skin and then blasts forth, exploding from the inside out like a thousand blue suns.

I'm blinded by it. I'm sure we all are.

When my eyesight comes back, there are fresh crystals *everywhere*. I mean, it's like we're on the North Pole all of a sudden. Blue-tinted white crystals cover every inch of the Mercury. They line the stage, the empty seats, the walls, the mezzanine, and even fill the hole in the roof. Everything is bright now, like Urma banished the summertime and made an ice cave.

The crystals even cover me and everyone else. I look around at my mom, V, Too Tall, Sol, and Sula—all of us are practically wearing suits of armor made of crystal that hold us fast to the crystalized floor. We're each like a human stalagmite.

I can't move. The crystal is like cold hard steel. My arms, my legs, my knees, my jaw are all locked up tight. It's even hard to breathe. The Lost and Found is on the floor between my feet, partially covered in crystal. I can just barely look down to see the Watch of 13. The hand inches to forty-five minutes away from the thirteenth hour. Mint appears from stage right. He stalks in gingerly on the crystal floor, careful with each step.

"You were right, Urma," he says. "The boy came through." He surveys the stage and forces a pleased smile. But I'm not so convinced this is what he had in mind.

Behind him, four more of his scarred goons haul out

the heavy, hog-tied bodies of my two uncles. Long Fingers and Crooked Eye groan and cuss into the gags across their mouths, hands twined tight behind their backs. Urma's goons drag my dad's brothers along the crystal floor and toss them beneath Urma's feet like they're hefting trash bags. My uncles struggle against their bindings until they accept it's hopeless.

The crystals hold me rock-still, but my stomach is doing backflips. A rage ignites in my chest. But I can't call out. My lips are clamped shut.

Urma Tan, still hovering in the blue light, is now slowly rotating like a figure in a snow globe. There's a serene smile on her face. The way someone looks when they're eating an insanely good meal. Mint and the goons just watch, entranced. Like they're waiting for words or a message. She doesn't seem to notice that any of us are here. I'm not entirely sure what's happening. It seems like this hunger for Realm energy has consumed her completely.

I think about how I held her crystal back at her place on Torrini Boulevard. Urma was turning gray. I dropped the crystal and left it for her because she needed it to live. Now it's like she just lives to feed. If I hadn't given her back the crystal, could I have stopped all of this from happening?

I want to help my uncles up. I just want to *move*, so bad. I want to free my friends.

But I feel the energy draining from me. I'm stuck thinking about how wrong things have gone. And how it's all my fault. The final pieces click into place. It was *Urma* who put the code on the marquee. She was around Maestro and Dad, she must have known the code from way back when. Then she must have found the box. But she couldn't open it. She didn't have the Watch of 13. She needed Long Fingers for that. Or, as it turned out, me. She said she wanted the box to recharge her crystals. But we did her one better and built her a whole portal and went and opened it for her. So she could do . . . *this*. Just drink and consume endlessly, not caring if she breaks our world.

I was so blind, so fixed on being the hero and rescuing my father, I ruined everything he sacrificed himself for.

I watch the energy gush from the Mirror.

I wonder, *Did she do this last time?*

Was she consuming the energy when my dad broke the Mirror?

As these thoughts lay me low, I realize I have to resist. *It's not over*, I tell myself. *It's not over.* It's the only thought that keeps me from giving up. *It can't be over. I won't let it be.*

My finger moves.

The index finger on my Realm hand.

It begins with that little finger wiggle. *It's not over,* I repeat to myself. The crystal that formed around my Realm hand cracks. I feel the hard crystal split down my arm. There's suddenly space around my hand. My fingers flex and it can *move*. I make a fist and summon all the concentrated force that I can manage. I put all that bad feeling of letting everyone down into that fist. I let it build and build. All the disappointment in myself. How I let down V and Tall, and all their faith in me. And Sol, who somehow believed in me, too. How I broke Mom's heart. And how bad I just missed Pop.

I see the clock click closer to 13 . . .

And I let it all go.

I flex my hand flat and shatter the crystal surrounding me into tiny pieces. I can somehow feel every little shard in my Realm hand, like they're all tied to strings looped around my fingers. I feel them like extensions of me. I hold each shard suspended, like hail frozen in time. I feel as though they're waiting for my direction. So I send them at Urma.

Every last crystal shard flies at her like a maelstrom.

She waves her hand and the shards come to an abrupt halt.

I fall to the crystal floor, drained, and land on top of the Lost and Found. I realize that was *all* of my power. And she stopped it cold.

She turns to me with a feline grin. I hear Mint's hoarse laughter. With a flick of her fingertips, she sends the sharp shards right back at me.

I hug my arms around the Lost and Found, and leap in the only direction I can.

Straight into the Mirror.

I'M FLOATING.

There's no ground beneath me, but also nothing pulling me down. I'm just *there*. Momentum carried me through the Mirror, and then I stopped. I'm in empty Realm space, hovering in the air, if air is even what you'd call it. I imagine this is what it's like with no gravity. I'm not even sure what I'm breathing, or whether I'm breathing. I just seem to be alive somehow.

I turn back the way I came. I can see through to the other side of the Mirror. There's Urma, looking after me. She doesn't like that I got away, but she's too busy feeding to care. There's Mom, V, and Tall, all locked up in crystal, with Sula and Sol. There's Long Fingers and Crooked Eye, tied up near Urma Tan's feet. And there's Mint and crew, looking dumbfounded. Their eyes are all on the Mirror.

I know what I need to do. Break the glass from the inside, like Dad did. But I don't know how. There isn't exactly a rock around for me to throw through the glass. Really, from this side it doesn't even look like *glass*. It just looks like a portal to reality itself, wreathed by blue flame.

I am in the Realm. I see other portals lit up in the darkness ahead of me, like mirrors tinted electric blue. They must lead to other echoes, other realities, just like Black Herman told me in the graveyard. Two portals are close to me. One is moving closer and the other is shrinking. The rest trail off forever, repeating and repeating until they're just like far-off stars.

I realize Dad must have been here, in this strange space, when he tried to return to us. Is his portal closed for good? I glance down at the clockface on Magician's Lost and Found. The little hand is maybe thirty minutes from the 13.

When my hand went through this box, I started a new echo and put Pops on the clock. Wherever his echo is in here, time will be up at the thirteenth hour. I might never be able to find him again.

As I stare from one portal to the next, I realize I'm

falling toward them. I have no clue what's up or down. I thought I was vertical, but it turns out I'm horizontal. My stomach feels like it's somewhere near my throat.

As I get closer, I can see through the entrance of each portal. It's like I'm looking through a window into someone's house. Except these aren't houses, these are echoes, new dimensions created the moment the Realm opens. Within the bigger portal to my right is the Mercury, dark and dormant, blanketed in ash and dust. It's just as it was yesterday, when I opened the Magician's Lost and Found. Within the shrinking portal to my left, speeding farther away, is the Mercury, bright and alive, a packed house, and a show on the stage . . . *The Mercury of four years and six months ago. It's not gone. Not yet.* Then I crash through the larger portal and I tumble to the Mercury's stage, covered in dust.

It takes a moment to orient myself. I'm in the Mercury. From *yesterday*. Well, not actually yesterday, but a copy of it. The Realm's echo of yesterday. It's a dead ringer for yesterday, anyway. Same shadows slanting across the audience. Same sunbeam spotlighting the stage. Same eerie quiet that's heavy with shows past.

I realize this is what Black Herman was talking about. I'm in an echo, and if I want to ride to another echo, to where my father disappeared, I must jump through this echo that I created when I opened the Magician's Lost and Found.

I glance to the Lost and Found in my hands right now. The clock says twenty-two minutes to go.

I hear someone coming. *Who's that now?* I wonder. *Mint?* I leap down to the orchestra section and stash the Lost and Found under one of the dusty seats and hide behind it. The footsteps come closer.

"Oh, hey, King. There you are."

It's Too Tall. He sees clear over my hiding spot. He's looking right at me.

My heart is beating a million times a second. *What do I do? What do I say?*

"Oh, um. Hey, Tall," comes out of my mouth.

"Why you hiding like that?" he asks. I realize *he* was expecting to see me.

"Um, I dunno," I say. "Just got spooked, I guess. Man, this place is creepy, huh?"

"You said it, man. Jeez."

I try to remember exactly what happened yesterday. Where am I now? Well, not me, but the other *me*, the Realm me.

"How'd you get those clothes?" asks Tall with his eyebrows scrunched up.

"Oh, I just, like, had these on, under my other shirt and shorts, you know?"

"Um, what? My dude, it's like eighty degrees outside."

"Well, I run cool, is all that is."

I close my eyes, realizing how lame all this sounds.

He looks at me like I'm from Pluto.

But it doesn't matter at all if this Too Tall thinks I'm crazy. He's a Realm copy and not the real Too Tall at all. Just like Urma. I just need to get to the *echo* before the clock runs out. But how?

Think, Kingston.

Another portal. That's how. That's the only way. Riding echoes. Like Black Herman said.

I opened the portal yesterday. The one that made this whole echo happen to begin with. I created the portal by accident when my hand went through the Lost and Found. I didn't see it, but then again, I was *under* all six-foot-plus of Too Tall at the time.

When the last portal opened up, you need to be there, and jump through. That's what Black Herman said. Riding echoes.

I look up at Too Tall, and panic hits me like a punch to the chest.

Yesterday, I opened the portal when I stuck my hand

into the Lost and Found, and Tall *fell on me*. But what happens if he's distracted, and doesn't fall on me, because I'm here talking to him?

"Um, Tall, have you been up on the stage?" I ask, my voice trembling with nerves.

He shakes his head.

"You see that wild mural up there?"

"Nah, it's cool?"

"Very."

He leaps up onstage. I grab the Lost and Found from where I stashed it under the seat. I hold it behind my back as I follow Too Tall. "Man, I already wrecked these kicks when I came down that chute," he says, eyeing the dusty stage steps as he climbs. "You know, I haven't even worn these OGs but three times. Dead-stocked out the box." He shakes his head.

Exactly what the real Too Tall would say. These Realm copies are *identical but they're not real*. So that means *I'm* somewhere down under this stage. Another me. The thought gives me a chill.

I see the open trapdoor in center stage, in front of him. I know he was looking at the mural when he fell on me.

"*Wow*, that's your pops, right? Man, that mural is excellent," he says, eyes fixed on the scene of my dad and

Maestro squared off as his feet keep walking, keep walking toward the door . . .

Get ready, I tell myself.

"*Yooo—*" he howls.

Sure enough, Tall slips and falls into the trap.

Here's my chance.

I watch from above as Tall crashes into me—well, the *other* me—and my hand is jolted into the box.

Blue light shoots from the box. From above, I see the infinite reflections of the Realm. This is the moment I created a new echo. I must jump. My echo self falls backward and pulls his hand from the box. A blue burning energy outlines the box. There's only so much space in this trap beneath the stage. Most of the portal seems to be under the stage where I can't see. I can't even make out what the portal leads *to*. There's only a little corner I could jump through.

It couldn't have been open for long, since I didn't even see it when I'd opened it. So here goes—it's my only shot.

I hold on to the Lost and Found and leap—

And I hit the side of the trap on the way down and land in the blue flame around the portal's edges.

AN EXPLOSION OF energy courses through me. My mind feels like it's breaking into little bits, spreading out, traveling like lightning, and forming back together. I'm able to think and see, but not feel. I'm not aware of having hands or arms or feet or even breath. But I do see things.

I see the Mercury, once again. But like I've never seen it before.

I'm on the stage. Maestro is just a few feet away. Pop is behind him. Urma is about to step through the Mirror. And I'm the Mirror. Literally standing in the Mirror.

Am I stuck in it? In between echoes?

I remember something Black Herman said. *When*

you ride echoes, you can miss and get stuck in the portal itself. I look out at a packed house. Everyone, even the ushers in the balcony, have their eyes glued to the performance. The lights are so bright, I have trouble seeing every face in the crowd, at first. But then I find the seat, center orchestra, three rows back. There's Mom, and there's me.

A good four and a half years younger. Smaller, hair much shorter. I look like a blank page.

I expect to see myself alert and concerned. That's how I remember it. I was one of the first to realize that something wasn't quite right. I remember the look on Dad's face. I remember the tremor of what was about to happen before it happened.

But it doesn't go down like that. There's no tremor. There's no look on Dad's face. There's no look on my face. I mean, I'm watching the show, but watching normal, like I'm waiting for a cool trick, just like everyone else.

I must have twisted it up in my memory. I must have told myself that I saw it coming.

I reach to pull myself out of the Mirror and step onstage, but my hand hits the glass from the inside. I can't reach into the scene in front of me. I look down at the Watch. *Ten minutes and time's up.*

And now, I'm stuck here, too. Does that mean when the portal closes, I won't make it back?

So instead of Dad stuck in the Realm forever, it's *me* . . .

There's Urma, staring into the Mirror. This is a different Urma, though. She looks scared. This must be the original Urma, Sula's mom. No cold eyes or purplish veins running through her neck. She makes eye contact, for just a brief second. She looks confused.

Then I look behind the curtain, stage left, and see the other Urma. She's visible for a moment, only to me, as far as I can tell. She's stepped from the cover of the curtain and makes this move with her hand like she's throwing a baseball.

Before I can take it all in, Sula's mom flies toward me, right into the Mirror. She goes through me, like a gust of wind that should knock me backward, only I can't seem to go backward. The force of her passing blurs my vision for a moment.

She's through the Mirror and gone behind me.

The other Urma starts drawing a flash of blue light to her behind the curtain.

If memory serves, Maestro is next.

From this angle, I can see the panic in his face. I guess he didn't expect Urma to go through the Mirror. He doesn't hesitate. He jumps through the Mirror now, too. He doesn't even seem to notice me. Am I that hard to see, somehow? He passes through me and I feel the force of it again as my vision gets cloudy.

Now it's Dad's turn.

I always remember him giving me that wink in the audience. The one so quick you barely know you saw it, like the flap of a wing. But I don't think he winks at me in my seat.

He sees me in the Mirror.

He's on the stage and he makes eye contact with me in the glass. He looks concerned. Then he jumps in.

Only he doesn't go right through me like Urma and Maestro. He catches me by my left hand, and I hold on and pull him toward me, like I'm saving him from falling through an open door. He stands beside me like he's joined me in the reflection.

"King," he says. Dad is just as he was four years ago, to a T. I know he's a Realm echo. He's not my real dad. But he looks just like him. Acts just like him. Probably thinks just like him. And he says, "What're you doing here?"

"I'm here to rescue you."

"Rescue *me*? I'm here to rescue *you*," he says, and knocks on the glass surface in front of us, testing its strength.

"You saw me," I say.

"In the reflection," he confirms.

I'm wondering, *Did he see me, back then? Did the real Pops see me when he leapt through? Is that even possible? Did I somehow show up in the Mirror four and a half years ago? Is that the logic of the Realm? Look forward and backward, it's all the same.*

"Pops, did you jump through to break the Mirror and close the portal? Or to save me?" I ask.

He seems surprised by the question. "It's a twofer, I guess."

I realize he couldn't possibly know what my real dad saw or didn't see. He only knows what he sees.

He's staring over my shoulder. "What's that behind you?"

What *is* behind me? I've been staring at the stage this whole time. I turn around and see.

There's the blue outline of a portal, only it seems far away. Inside the portal, I see the Mercury of *now*. In real time. With Urma Tan drinking Realm energy. With V and Tall, with my uncles and mom, with Sol and Sula, all trapped in crystal. The portal is getting smaller, almost like looking through a telescope. It's fading away with each tick of the clock.

I turn again. There's the Mercury of *then*. There's the packed house erupting in flames. Everyone panicking. My four-years-ago self holds my mom's hand and runs down the aisle.

My dad and I—we're *inside* the portal, straddling these two realities. In the far distance, there's the reflection of my reality, the Mercury of now. My family encased in crystals, Urma lit up like a blue goddess. Slowly pulling farther and farther away.

I look at the Lost and Found in my hands. The watch clicks four minutes away from the 13.

"King?" says my dad.

"That's my time," I say. "That's Mom. That's our family. They're really trapped. They're in trouble."

"King, don't be scared," he says.

"How do I help them?" I ask.

"What went wrong?" he asks.

"Did you know there's a second Urma Tan? A Realm copy?" I ask. I realize I can ask him all the questions I want to ask my real dad. Their answers would probably be exactly the same.

"*Yes,*" he says, amazed. "I just found out. Maestro confessed about the double-Urma act. He told me that the Realm Urma was draining the life from his kids. He convinced me to help him open this portal to send her back to the Realm. Only, something went wrong, and I'm the fail-safe. I have to make sure the Realm is closed. I wish we had time for you to tell me all about your life now. But you've got your own emergency."

"Urma. The Realm Urma. She's opened a portal."

"I see it," he says, looking over my shoulder. "It's fading fast."

He glances at the Lost and Found in my hands. "Good. You've got my box, and my watch." He looks closer at the Watch of 13. "Not much time left at all. King, you and I have the same problem."

There's a portal open in his reality, and a portal open in my reality. "I guess we do," I say. "With the same Urma."

"Just let me help get you out of here," says Dad.

"You know how I can get home?" I ask.

"Well, it's tricky, you might say. But I have an idea."

"Wait, Dad—I gotta ask. How do I stop Urma?"

"I sure wish I'd been able to stop her. But send Urma back to the Realm. Otherwise, she won't ever stop. She'll keep drawing the Realm through the open portal until your world, the real world, drowns. She belongs in the Realm."

"One more question," I say. "Will you come with me?"

"Come with you? Into your reality? I can't do that, Kingston."

"But why?"

"Don't you see? What's happened to Urma could happen to me. I wish we could spend some time together, King. You know I do. But you belong in your world, and me in mine," says Dad.

"But you *left* our world. You never make it back, Pop."

"I never make it back?"

"Not in four and a half years. But I never gave up on you. I came into the Realm to get you." I want to tell him everything. About my Realm hand, how I can do real magic, about how I met Black Herman, about Mom and the King's Cup café and V and Tall and I even want to tell him about Sol's murals and Sula's universe-size eyes.

"And that's why you're stuck here now?" he asks.

"Yeah."

Hearing that seems to crush him. "I'm so sorry, Kingston. I'm sorry I had to leave. I'm sorry it's taking me so long to get back, that you and your mom had to go all these years without me, that you had to come after me." He lowers his eyes and they land on the Watch of 13. "Ah, King. You're running out of time. The least I can do is set you free."

I look down at the Watch. Sure enough, thirty seconds to go. Thirty more clicks of the big hand and the little hand will hit 13. "But you won't come?" I ask.

"I'll make it back one day, Kingston. No matter what."

Pop takes the Magician's Lost and Found in his hands. He raises the box over his head. "When I say jump, take my hand, and jump toward the portal behind you," he says. "When I break the glass, that should free you. Your momentum from the jump should take you home."

And he smashes the box down, hard, just to my right.

"Jump!"

And I take his hand in my left hand and jump.

I feel the shards of glass falling down, all around me.

I feel like I'm the shards.

Like I'm breaking up into bits again, spreading out, traveling like lightning, and forming back together.

It's like being in the trunk of a car as it drives over speed bumps and *whams* into ditches.

I move through the portal, and spill headfirst onto the crystalized floor of the Mercury.

I CAN BREATHE again. Smell again. Feel again.

I make quite an entrance, coming back in through the Mirror the way I came, the Magician's Lost and Found tumbling through the Mirror after me.

Urma is there, drinking the blue Realm energy with a thirst that has no end. The blue light is glowing from her eyes, and it's like she can't even see me.

I concentrate all of my strength into my Realm hand. I can feel the energy burning through this Mirror. I feel like I can direct it. Control it.

I close my eyes, and I can sense Urma, hovering above the crystal. She feels light, somehow. As though I can just push . . .

"Where's she going?" Mint asks as she sails toward the portal.

Urma's eyes snap and she's suddenly aware of what's happening around her.

"No!" she shrieks, and halts in midair right in front of the Mirror, reaching a clawing hand toward me.

I'm only a couple feet away from her, willing her through. "Go back, Urma," I say. "You belong in the Realm."

"I need to *feed*," she says, resisting my effort to push her into the Mirror. This isn't about her survival anymore. Her appetite is bottomless.

I realize, Urma in or out, I *need* to destroy that portal. The Magician's Lost and Found is open at my feet.

And I think back to what Dad did.

He used the box.

He smashed the Mirror from the inside with the Magician's Lost and Found.

I turn to the box. With my Realm hand glowing blue, I raise the box in the air, and send it hurling at Urma. It crashes into her chest and carries her through the Mirror with a shout.

Once Urma and the Lost and Found have cleared to the other side, I turn my wrist and pull my hand into a fist and will the box to come back to me.

It *shatters* the Mirror from the inside into a hundred bits, raining broken glass into the crystal floor like a waterfall.

The place goes dark. The blue light is gone. The crystals all fade to black.

I blink and my eyes slowly adjust. I reach to the dark crystals surrounding my family and shatter them with one push of my Realm hand. The crystals pulverize into dust. Then I turn to my uncles. Mint and his goons block the way.

"It's over," I say. "Your bootleg goddess is back where she belongs. Go and be on your way. Unless you want me to send you." Without realizing it, my Realm hand brightens the stage with a blue glow.

Mint digs a cold look into me. His nostrils flare. He and I both know he's got no hand to play. "Okay, boys. Let's be out."

One by one, they peel off and drop down off the stage. They make their way across the crystal-slicked aisles and toward the front entrance.

"King, that was amazing!" I hear as V tackles me and wraps me up in a hug.

"You the *man*, King!" says Tall, taking my hand in his. I feel him stuff something in my palm.

It's my *glove*.

Very slick. V's hug turned me just so no one could see.

"Thanks, guys," I say, slipping the glove back on my Realm hand. My hand was glowing when I came through the Mirror, so maybe my mom didn't see that it's actually invisible now. "But I didn't get Dad back."

"But King," says V, "you jumped through the Mirror—and *you* came back!"

With a little help from a Realm version of the man himself, of course, I think, but I keep it to myself. There's too much to explain, for now.

Sol gives me a big high five. He's got this goofy smile, like he's drinking a chocolate milkshake or something. Sula smiles at me with those big eyes. I hold out my hand and she takes it. Respect.

My uncles' bindings are actually tougher to break than the depowered crystals. My Realm hand doesn't really work on them. I pick a shard up off the floor and use its edge to cut the layers of twine wrapped around their wrists.

Uncle Crooked gives me a big, blubbery hug. "My boy, I'm *so* proud."

Long Fingers takes me by the hand and shakes it, looking in my eye and beaming. "I thought she had us." Then he looks at the shard I'm holding. "You and me got to talk. Boy, do we need to talk."

"We will, Unc," I say with a quick wink. It's sorta my version of my dad's wink. "Soon. Got lots to tell you."

I turn, and there's my mom. She's been hanging back, just watching. There's so many emotions knotted up in her face, I don't know whether to laugh, cry, hug, or run. I just open my mouth and say, "Mom. I am so sorry."

She shudders like she's about to cry.

"Did you see him, in that Mirror somewhere?" she asks.

"Yeah," I say. "I saw him. I got to touch him."

She hugs me. "I'm sorry, Kingston. I just wanted to protect you," she says.

"I know, Ma. I know."

"Does this mean he won't ever come back?" she asks.

"He'll come back. One day," I say. "He told me so himself."

I look at the husk of the busted Mirror and the shards piled on the floor. It looks a lot like the last Mirror from four and a half years ago, but no fire this time. All I set out to do was bring him back, and I don't have him back, once again. Instead, in a weird way, I finished his trick—though it wasn't ever really a trick. We both jumped through that Mirror, but I'm the only one who made it back. He was almost here, just now, so close. Now he's back somewhere in that *Realm*, that series of strange magic places and echoes—that *Echoverse*, I guess, riding echoes. I have so much to tell him, and now add that an echo of him saved me. And saved us all.

EPILOGUE

MY POPS USED to say I'd have to choose my own path someday. That I could only walk with him so far, and then I would have to decide which way to go.

It's been three weeks since I saw him in the echo or the Realm, or whatever you call that place. It's like somewhere I just visited for the day.

I can see the massive obsidian from our street. They're calling it the Black Rock of BK, formerly the Mercury Theater. Now it's a dark crystal almost a block long and six stories high. You can see it just peeking over the buildings like a setting black sun. Some news vans showed up, people started selling T-shirts—our neighborhood became a destination. Like Stonehenge or those Easter Island statues or crop circles.

The new normal—that's what Ma calls it.

It's also been good for business. We officially went with the name King's Cup. Ma put a King of Hearts on the logo. After everything we went through, she understands that magic will always be a part of our family. She's got a line of customers. All the worry about the brownstone and "foreclosure"—well, we're open, and sometimes way past four. Mom seems happy.

Today, we've got a good crowd. Crooked Eye is balancing a plate of fresh pastries.

"Customers," he says with a smile.

I grab some quarters one of the customers left on the table and flip them a few times over my knuckles, looking out the window.

Too Tall barrels inside. He's talking before I even get a chance to say hello.

"King, King—there's something you gotta see," he says, and almost runs over V.

"If it isn't Bigfoot himself," Veronica says as she drops off a few coffees to some customers.

"V, come look," Tall says. "Miss James, you too. All of you."

"We're a little busy here, Eddie," Ma tells him.

"Trust me, it won't take long," Too Tall says.

Long Fingers is ringing someone up at the register. "Go ahead, we got this," Long Fingers tells my mom.

He's been getting out a lot more since that night. He even got himself a haircut. He's less wolfman these days, but I still hear him in his lab tinkering into the late hours of the night.

"This way, this way," Tall says, motioning for us to see the back side of our building. We turn left down the alley and stop cold.

It's a new mural. The kid is at it again. And he's getting better. We haven't seen a new one of these since that night.

It's the inside of the Mercury, every detail just the way I remember it from last month. The pigeons nested near the holes in the ceiling. The charred stage, the broken light bulbs. In the middle of the stage is the Mirror. Inside the Mirror is Pops. Classic Pops, dressed to the nines. He's holding the Magician's Lost and Found in one hand. His other hand holds a hand that disappears at the wrist by the edge of the Mirror.

"It just appeared last night," Tall says.

V rests her hand on his shoulder. "Give them a minute."

Ma steps forward and stares up at the mural. She doesn't say a word. She takes my hand.

I look at her and I look at Pops in the Mirror within the mural.

He saved Echo City. Saved me, and reality as we know it.

Then I feel something grab my hand. My phantom hand.

And I look up at the mural. I swear the painting of him winks at me.

I look to Ma. Somehow, we're all here now. All three of us.

I'm holding both my parents' hands at once, across dimensions, for the first time in four years, seven months, and eight days.

Turn the page for a sneak peek
at Kingston's next adventure

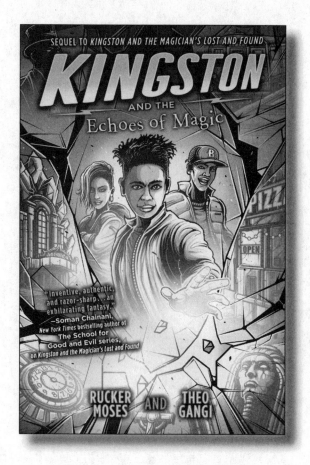

I'VE BEEN HERE before.

Every sight and every sound feel as familiar as yesterday.

Whenever that was.

We're riding the subway home from the Barclays Center. I got a seat by the window. It's Friday evening, and Christmas is just days away. The Brooklyn Nets just lost to the New York Knicks. *The thum-da-doom* of the tracks rumbles in my bones. All the heads of all the passengers bob to the rhythm. My eyes are drifting shut. I'm sleepy from all the shouting and popcorn eating and Milly Rocking during time-outs. I stare out the dark glass. The tunnel speeds along, and sharp dashes of light blast by like laser beams.

The subway window reflects the inside of the car. I can see my best bud Too Tall, my primo prima Veronica, and my uncle Crooked Eye, dead asleep and snoring. And there's myself looking right back at me. High cheekbones. Hair twists growing long up top.

The subway lights flash off. It's pitch-dark, and then light again.

As we roll into Ricks Street, my uncle's eyes snap open like he's got some kind of sixth subway sense, and he's awake and talking.

But I know what he's going to say before he says it.

Let's go, sleepyfaces.

"Let's go, sleepyfaces. It's our stop."

You're one to talk, Unc.

"You're one to talk, Unc," says Veronica, standing and steadying herself as the train slows to a stop. "You snore louder than the express train."

As we exit the train, file through the turnstiles, and climb the staircase to the street, I'm thinking about how the first thing I'll see on the horizon is the Black Rock of BK, as the news started calling it. The hard crystal rock that's encased what was formerly the Mercury Theater and is now the main tourist attraction of Echo City. There's even this federal Omega team from the government that's investigating it. They've got tents set up around the Mercury, and they wear these orange vests with the letter *O* on the back. I guess they're trying to figure out what it is and what it's doing here and why all the blackouts, but they can't explain it. I know because I happen to be one of the very few who actually sorta can.

This past summer, a big rift from another dimension called the Realm heaped out tons of raw energy that immediately crystalized into a huge, towering rock, like a mountain right smack-dab on the streets of Brooklyn.

I can imagine how the rock will look when I get up to the street—the sunset glowing pink and the black crystal looking down on the brownstone roofs, shadow long in the streets like it's on stilts.

Once I reach aboveground and check the skyline, I see how exactly right I was. The Black Rock of BK is just how I pictured. But only for a moment.

The sun soon settles all the way down, and the darkness grows and spills into the shadows of alleys and buildings. Then the lights go out. Blackness pours over us like somebody knocked an ink bottle over on Echo City.

Then the streetlamps pop back on with a flicker.

"Whoa," says Too Tall with a squint. "These outages are a trip, boy." He zips his bubble coat up and pulls his skullcap over his ears, like the lights going out made it colder somehow.

I wait a second and then raise my gloved hand.

"Let there be . . . *dark*," I say as the streetlights dim and go out again, the way they do when you're close to the Mercury.

It feels even darker than last time.

"King, you're really freaking us out, you know? If you're doing this, could you stop, please?" he asks, looking at my gloved hand. "What I mean is"—he clears his throat and drops his voice an octave deeper—"I'm not scared of the dark at all."

"Not at all," says Veronica.

But I'm not doing it. I just know when it will happen.

Because I've been here before.

ONE THING I like about when the lights go out in the city: You can actually see the stars. Most of the time, I forget about them. In Brooklyn, there's so much to see at eye level: stores, cars, outfits, faces, WALK/DON'T WALK signs, bus stops, buildings, brownstones, yards, stairs, doorways. There's even a ton to see when you look down. For one, people's feet—Brooklyn's sneaker game is out of control. Sometimes you just need to look down because the sidewalks crack different. Trees *do* grow in Brooklyn; they grow big and the roots break the sidewalk, so you'd better watch your step. You never really look up. There's no reason to. With the glare of streetlamps and holiday lights and the dome of smog, you usually can't see the stars even if you want to.

But since the outages, I've been looking up more and more. Especially now that it's winter and it gets dark so early. It reminds me of when we used to visit Grandpa Freddy in Georgia. You could really see the stars out there. Pops used to stare up at them. He'd call it Little Big Sky.

I look up now and think, *When the lights go out, Brooklyn's got its own Little Big Sky.* Thousands of tiny lights surrounded by infinite blackness. I don't know the stars too well. But I look for the ones I do know—the three points of Orion's Belt. Something about it always makes me think of the Realm.

Maybe it's because Pops is in the Realm, and I want to get him home.

Or maybe it's because of what it was like when I was in the Realm.

I jumped from echo to echo to echo, like the three

stars in Orion's Belt, and in between was black and vast, like the space that surrounds the stars.

Looking out into space, I feel small. Not just me, but my house and family and my block and city, even. Everything I know is so small compared with the humongous galaxy.

But another part of me feels like, *I was in the night sky*. Like, *out there* in some wild interdimensional convergence of outer or inner space. And that makes me feel big. Big as the whole universe sometimes.

ACKNOWLEDGMENTS

FIRST, THIS BOOK wouldn't have been possible without the original creator and third star in the SunnyBoy constellation, Michael White. Big thanks to Jane Startz, our shepherd; her faith in us and vision for what we had was beyond our own perception. To our editor, Stacey Barney: thank you for taking a shot on us, bringing the band together, making us better writers, and making the world we dreamed up greater than we could have imagined. With gratitude to our parents for putting books and ideas into our heads and hands. Love and endless appreciation to our wives, who carry and support us with their time, love, and energy. Thanks to Uncle Pat, our earliest reader, for sharing your wonderful, creative brain. Thanks to Dr. James and Mary for all the great magic books and space talk. Shout-out to Ted B. for lifting us up and making us believe in our ideas. Thank you to Sienne for the laughs, the drawings, and bringing the happiness all day, every day. To St. Francis College's MFA program for your creativity, your community, your courage, and all your favorite Cs. Big ups to the SunnyBoy crew for rocking the chairs on the best front porch in the universe. What would we be without the endless magical conversations, friendships, and adventures? To Ant for being a brother like no other. To the great Black magicians: your due will come. Most importantly, thanks to our kids—your lives are our greatest story.

© Zak Forsman

RUCKER MOSES is the pen name of Craig S. Phillips and Harold Hayes, Jr. They both hail from Atlanta and started telling stories together at the University of Georgia. They've been nominated for three Emmys for writing in a children's program and have written for TV shows based on books by R. L. Stine and Christopher Pike. They also make virtual reality experiences and own a production company named SunnyBoy Entertainment. In no particular order, their favorite things to write about are ninjas, magic, space, and abandoned amusement parks. When not doing all that, they are hanging with their wonderful families at home in Los Angeles and Atlanta.

© Kamilah Black Gangi

THEO GANGI is a novelist and writing teacher based in Brooklyn. He's written several acclaimed novels and short stories, and he's worked on shows for Netflix. He writes far-out adventures that happen right next door. He directs the MFA program at St. Francis College and lives with his wife, young son, and their dog.